About the Author

Polis Loizou is a novelist, playwright, filmmaker and performance storyteller. Born and raised in Cyprus, he moved to the UK in 2001. His debut novel *Disbanded Kingdom* was published in 2018 and went on to be longlisted for the Polari First Book Prize. His second novel, *The Way it Breaks*, was published in 2021. His short stories and creative non-fiction have been published in various anthologies and literary journals. Having co-founded an award-winning theatre troupe, with which he has toured the UK festival circuit, Polis has delved deeper into the world of folk storytelling to perform a couple of acclaimed solo shows. He currently lives in Nottingham with his husband and cats.

A Good Year

POLIS LOIZOU

Fairlight Books

First published by Fairlight Books 2022

Fairlight Books
Summertown Pavilion, 18–24 Middle Way, Oxford, OX2 7LG

A CIP catalogue record for this book is available from the
British Library

1 2 3 4 5 6 7 8 9 10

ISBN 978-1-914148-05-7

www.fairlightbooks.com

Printed and bound in Great Britain by Clays Ltd.

Designed by Sara Wood

Illustrated by Sam Kalda

To better times

Κόκκινη κλωστή δεμένη,
στην ανέμη τυλιγμένη,
δώσ' της κλώτσο να γυρίσει,
παραμύθι ν' αρχινίσει

Red thread,
wound around the spinning wheel,
give it a kick to get it turning,
for a story to get going

—One of the traditional ways to start a tale in
the Greek-speaking world

FIRST DAY OF CHRISTMAS

She'd heard the story from her father, who'd heard it from his father, who'd heard it from his grandfather.

On the outskirts of the village, old Yakoumis came face to face with one of the creatures. It was after vespers on the twelve days. The night was black as molasses, and the wind that shook the bushes turned your head into a block of ice. And there, where the road curved down towards the towns, where the edge of the track tapered into a forest of pines, there at the well from which the old man raised a bucket of water, came a voice, thin but sharp as a needle.

Which way to your village? it said.

Yakoumis turned to find a thing that might have been a baby. A clump of black hair it was. In the light of the torch, its limbs unfolded like those of a newborn foal stretching into life.

— Over there, said Yakoumis, pointing towards the church.

Will you take me?

— For the love of God! Of course I will.

But Yakoumis the cobbler was no simpleton; he was a good Christian, and knew at once what this being was. As it extended its hairy hand to his, the cobbler reached for the piece of string he kept in his pocket. It was the method his father had taught him.

Thank you, said the creature.

Yakoumis grabbed its hand, the kalikantzaro wincing and stifling growls as the string pulled tight around its finger. If the old tales were true, and it appeared that they were, the creature was now his slave.

They walked by the light of the full moon towards the church, Yakoumis pulling his new possession along by the string. Imagine what the priest would say! Here he was, a humble cobbler, and he had captured the Devil's own. Might it be enough when the time came – would St Peter overlook his sins and admit him into heaven?

When they passed the coffee house, the creature was taller. When they passed the cemetery, the creature had a nose and lips and ears. By the time they reached the church, it could have been a grandson, covered in dirt from the mines. The door opened onto an empty church. The priest was gone. The village was asleep, every soul at home and in bed.

Yakoumis took the creature to his workshop. There, he tied the string in a knot around the leg of the bench.

— You will make boots from now on, he said to the kalikantzaro.

The thing nodded. But he requested a bowl of nuts and a glass of zivania.

And so, every night, Yakoumis would go to bed as the creature he'd fastened to his workbench produced pair after pair of hobnailed boots. And here was the thing: they were exquisite! The cobbler felt a simultaneous surge of pride and annoyance when the villagers remarked on the improved quality of his craft.

— Come and see the reason for it, he told some friends one afternoon.

So he took them to the workshop, where the men stood around staring at a vacant space.

— Here is my helper. Eh? What do you think?

The men glanced at one another.

— What are you talking about? There's nothing there.

Yakoumis looked hurt, then surprised, then angry.

— Are you blind? He's standing in the corner!

The men glanced at one another.

— For God's sake! spat Yakoumis. Who do you think's been having the nuts and zivania?

The men remained silent. They ought to have known that these beings, once caught and rendered harmless, can only be seen by their captors. From then on, Yakoumis said nothing more about the other being that shared his workshop. Every morning he would find on the bench a pair of brand-new boots, and an empty bowl and a drained glass.

One night, however, as he left his workbench for his bed, he forgot to snuff the candle. In the morning he discovered his error. By the candle's base was the end of the piece of string tied to the leg of the workbench, its tip singed and frayed. The creature was nowhere to be seen.

Yakoumis never saw it, or any others of its kind, again.

Of all the tales about the kalikantzari, it was this one that came to Despo when she woke on Christmas morning. Partly it was to do with her father's telling of it; his eyes went bright at the tying of the string, his lips curled at the mention of zivania. Since childhood her mind had cast him in the role of the cobbler. At the end of his days the telling, the fine-tuned performance, would be interrupted by a scratching cough, and he'd hack up blood into his handkerchief. He would always, for a moment, look dismayed, as if he'd had other plans, and then he'd remember to look happy for her. She was enamoured with him, and he with her. Instead of helping her mother to shell beans, she'd follow her father around the farm, and she would sit on his knee, his hand guiding her little fingers over the cows' udders, and she'd listen as he would tell her all his peculiar tales.

Perhaps he chose to tell this story of the cobbler instead of other ones so as to dampen her fear.

Some of the Christmas yarns were wicked, but in this one the creature was quickly subdued. There was no detail about its stench, sweat and urine, or the grotesqueness of its body – charcoal and hairy – or the limping about on the legs of donkeys. There was no unhinged laughter to the whine of fiddles through the pines, no trickery or violence visited on the old protagonist.

But the story ended with the creature vanished. And Despo knew, from the hundred other tales, that the creature had skipped back into the dark woods, back into that hole in the ground from which its kind emerged.

It was Christmas morning. She would keep the creatures at bay, from her mind, her house and, she thought, as her hand moved by instinct to her rounded stomach, her unborn child. To this being inside her, whom she prayed would be a boy, she whispered the words with which her father would end his tales:

— Don't worry, my love. It's all lies.

*

They'd been woken by the rooster. Despo waited for the third crow before she raised herself to dress for church. The bells called out through the morning mist, guiding the Christians of the village to the service. Today, the Saviour was born.

Rejecting the offer of her husband's arm, Despo took the step into the church, and then her place beside him in the pews. The tears slid down her cheeks; tears of gratitude and joy. In the candlelight the saints watched from their icons. The Virgin held her miracle baby, her rich blue robe enveloping them both like a womb. The priest's wine-rich chants spread through every body and washed over the ceiling, pillars and pews. But the corners of the altar were lost to the darkness. In another icon, the Saviour was an adult and bleeding at the wrists. There was a gash in his abdomen, a bloodied hole exposed to the world. Despo crossed herself, then crossed her stomach, too. Loukas was smiling at her, but in that sad way of his, as if he could only ever find joy in half a thing. The lamps in his head came on when their neighbours turned to kiss and hug them after the sermon. Happy Christmas and a good new year. May they all live to see the next.

— You'll drop any minute, said Anthou to Despo outside the church, afterwards. She was ten years older, so already had a dozen kids. Most had survived but one was blind, such was the will of God.

— Oof! As long as he's not born today, Despo replied.

— If he is, tie his hand to yours with wicker, so he won't run off with Them. Are you drinking chamomile?

— I am, but it's useless.

— Nonsense, it's good for the stomach. Keep at it.

Despo was already tired of Anthou's advice, but she nodded as she should. The woman was staring at the younger one's stomach with either distaste or concern, it wasn't clear.

Despo willed the baby to wait. Better after Epiphany. The kicking was growing impatient, the ache too much, but she would rather suffer it for twelve more days than risk the baby's life. Though she tried to sweep the kalikantzari from her mind, they lingered there, as they did in the shadows under bridges and in chimneys, waiting to come out. With God's blessing, she would remain unharmed. Her son would be granted the best chance at life.

— It's all lies, my love, she whispered. It's all lies.

*

They sat in silence at the table, where they imbibed the warmth of egg-and-lemon soup. It would only be the two of them till sunset, then they'd amble to his godparents' house for the feast. They'd been over there the night before, stuffing their faces with roasted hog and floating on conversation over the threshold of night. The salt of the meats had over-powered Despo, but she'd swallowed them down. It was only the changes of pregnancy taking their toll.

Christmas was her favourite time of year. Yes, the sun rose dim and was soon blown out, leaving them shivering against each other on the creaking bed, but these were days of pause, to count and enjoy their blessings. One of which came early on the morning of Christmas Eve; that scent of freshly baked bread encasing the village, when the ovens were lit and the housewives brought their pies and pastries and loaves. People laughed together over dinner. They reminisced about the departed, they clinked glasses of wine, and they looked forwards, beyond the pain of the past. Easter was the time for death and grieving, but now, celebrating the birth of Christ brought with it the hope of a new beginning, a prayer for a good year ahead.

— Bless your hands, said Loukas, as he set down his spoon to wipe his mouth on his sleeve.

— Are you full? There's more.

— I'm full. You made enough for six.

He was smiling, in his way.

— Eh, there'll soon be more of us, she said.

His smile wavered, then fell away. A darkness came over his eyes and mouth. And when he spoke, his voice weighed a ton:

— Next time, make less.

He rose from his seat and before she knew it the door was shut behind him. In a moment she saw his face behind the glass of the small square window. He was heading for the stable to feed the donkey. Then he was gone.

She had always been told to shut her mouth, and never in her life had she listened. It was lucky that her husband's hands, like her father's, almost never turned to fists. Any mention of the child appeared to provoke him, but she told herself it couldn't be that. It must have been the excess food she'd made. God willing, the grapes would be good this year, and their worries less frequent.

It wasn't the child; it couldn't be. What sort of man didn't want a son?

She distracted herself by cooking for the feast. She had promised her husband's godmother she would make koupepia, so she rolled up her sleeves and got to it, pausing only for the sudden shot of pain in her back. First she soaked the vine leaves. She let her hands linger in the bowl. Then she slammed the pig shoulder on the table, sliced off the tendons and tissue, and cut the meat into strips. With a knife in each hand she hammered at the strips until they became chunks, became cubes, became gravel.

What did it matter if Loukas never learned to love their child? She alone would lavish her son – and it would be a son – with more love than he'd ever need. It was what she had done for her siblings, before they were split up and scattered among the family, across the island. She would lather his fat little limbs with soap and kiss his soaking hair and hold him to her aching breast. And she would sing as she had to her brothers:

St Marina, maiden
You who lulls babies to sleep
Lull my baby too
My sweetest song

Her very own boy.

She minced the onion and tossed it in the oiled pan. The smell was like a blade. How her body had been changed, weakened. There was the always-bothered pelvis; the worn-out back; the swollen ankles; the blue veins in her legs, crawling upwards like fingers reaching for the child inside her. And there was every chance she might lose him. If not before birth then during, or shortly after. Five times the latter had happened to her mother, each of those children born only to die. After the salt had been rubbed on their limbs, after the ash had been dabbed on their lashes, after the holy water had blessed and cleansed them. And they were all in the ground before a week had passed, shocked asleep in their coffins. Their final breaths hung frozen around the house.

To think of all the little ones who'd died unbaptised… She prayed the angels had got to them before the Others did. There were stories of infections. Deformities. Children born with tails, or hands and feet clumped like donkeys' hooves.

Even if her son was lucky enough to live into his next year, he might die of a thousand things. Snakebite. Drowning. The consumption that had taken both her parents. The leprosy that had crumpled Loukas's mother and sent her away from him. Or the illness, worst of all, that had gripped his father.

She would not think of it. Instead, she would spoon parsley, rice, tomato, onion and pork into softened vine leaves, and wrap them as if against the cold. The koupepia sat together, swaddled in the pot.

She froze.

Her nails had grown. Despo knew to be careful of splitting them. It made the creatures stronger.

*

In the afternoon Loukas took his rifle to the woods. There among the snow-dusted pines he picked at berries on bushes, plump saffron mushrooms and fallen acorns, which he touched to his moustache and breathed in. Every so often he'd raise the gun and miss a bird. And sometimes, between the trees, he'd spot a squirrel darting off, or a vague other shape. Hairy face or hind legs – it was never slow enough to catch and discern. A goat or a mouflon.

All he wanted was to be out of the house.

There behind a fallen pine were some bushes, and behind them the creek where they'd found his father face-down in the water. He felt a vague ache in his heart. Six years. Almost without thinking, he fell back against a pine and stayed there, his breath going in and out, a panic seizing him as if he was about to expire. When the feeling passed he crossed himself, and gave up the hunt. He knelt to pick at the mushrooms on the floor. Grilled on charcoal, a squeeze of lemon: what more could you want?

An arm's length away from the tips of his fingers, there on the ground, was a wavy line. Glinting scales. He jumped. Up on his feet, rifle cocked, he aimed. But the serpent body was still, and the head, he realised, was missing. On closer inspection it had been chewed off; the snake was now a frayed rope. There was a rustling in the bushes. Loukas remembered his rifle, and fired. He heard the sound of feet, buried beneath the noise of running water. On the other side of the bushes was another snake. Again, it looked half eaten.

When he emerged from the woods, there where the road turned down towards the town, he bumped into the Englishman and his wife. They were dressed in their fine clothes, as usual. He wore a light jacket and she wore a skirt that stopped just below the knee. It wasn't only the length of the garment that was provocative, but the suggestion that the winter had no effect on this woman at all. Had she no soul? It was true what they said: these people were made of ice. In the sun they melted. Loukas picked out the word *Christmas* from the couple's greeting, but was too flummoxed by their sudden appearance to respond with anything more than a nod.

William, they called the man. Loukas had done some work in their orchards, at the mukhtar's recommendation. As they carried on walking, going who knew where on this day meant for God and family,

in a country a sea away from theirs, the Englishman
– hair the colour of fire and eyes the colour of ice,
like no one else in the village – turned back to smile
a second time.

*

Evening came and one of the children had been sent to
hurry them up. Despo carried her dish, negotiating the
slick cobbles in her boots, and Loukas took the mushrooms he'd gathered. His godfather, Nestoras, had gone
hunting, and on the table lit with oil lamps his prey lay
in a row, wings spread out as if to flaunt their plumage.
Whereas Loukas and Despo lived barely within the
limits of their home, like crabs in their shells, Nestoras
and his wife had a courtyard big enough to host a wedding, and an outer door to keep the roaming beggars
out. Some of them simply came in search of food and
shelter, others to steal what little you had.

The talk had turned to the Swedes, the group of
men with snow-blonde hair who'd come in search of
treasure. They'd been back and forth to the mountains
with their vehicles for months, making holes in the
ground but generally staying out of everyone's way.

— Have they finished?

— No, darling, it's their Christmas, too.

— Thank God.

— Eh, they've been digging around out there for six
months – they've gone beetroot. Who knows what for.

— Old cups and plates.

21

— Is that so? Go and smash that vase in the orchard, love, give them something to be pleased about.

— What the hell do they think they'll find?

— Something from the Ancients.

— What, here?

— Of course! Are you kidding? You think we don't have treasures in Cyprus?

— Now you tell me? So why am I picking olives like a fool? Get me a shovel and I'll dig up Aphrodite's hair-comb.

— Sit back and let me tell you about the Regina, and what she hid in her castle…

The party, indoors and out of the biting wind, was made up of Nestoras and his wife Agnoulla, their six children and eleven grandchildren, the youngest born not twelve weeks ago. It was a given that Loukas and Despo, the poor souls whose parents had already ended up either in the graveyard or in the asylum, were always invited. The fire crackled and spat, which the young ones found enticing. Outside, the fig tree loomed over the house, its leaves silently billowing.

Despo's lowered eyes slid over to her husband as he gorged on stewed rabbit and potatoes, okra in tomato sauce. Sucking the tips of his fingers, he praised the koupepia.

— Our Despina is the real treasure, said Agnoulla as she turned her gapped smile on Despo. God bless her hands.

Myrto, Agnoulla's eldest, reached out to touch Despo's swollen belly.

— And her stomach.

A sudden look of shock. Myrto's eyes went big and a smile opened her face.

— Oh, my darling – he's kicking…!

— I want to feel!

Myrto's own child ran to Despo, and struck his palm against her belly with such force that it made her wince.

— Careful, my love! The pregnant woman forced herself to speak with as much lightness as she could muster. Then she guided the boy to the flesh between his hand and her baby's feet. Holding his wrist, so easily encircled by her fingers, and seeing the joy in that mouth that was no bigger than a walnut, brought a tear to her eye. Another kick came, which made him laugh.

— Does it hurt?

— A little. But it's worth it.

Later, they ate the sweetmeats and pastries. There were Kiki's melomakarona, which had soaked up the syrup well but were sprinkled with so much cinnamon that Despo had to suppress a cough. There were Myrto's kourabiedes; perfect texture, just the right amount of rosewater. And, of course, there was Agnoulla's gennopitta, which the hostess had made annually since her first year of marriage. She always gave it an extra layer of pastry in the shape of a cross, its pattern and depth casting deep shadows in the low light.

One of the girls whined, because Myrto's son had tugged her hair.

— Stop that now! his father roared. Or I'll give you to the beggars.

Horrified, the boy hid behind a chair.

— No!

— Yes. And they'll break your legs, too. They get more money if you're broken.

— No! No!

— Kleanthis, for God's sake, my love! Don't say such things.

— I have to, Ma. You have to scare this one to shut him up.

— Let's not speak of things like that at the table. This is the Lord's day. We should be celebrating the miracle of birth.

Despo willed the conversation to change. And, thank God, it did. While the children played by the fire, tossing bones and eggshells into the flames and giggling, the adults picked at sweets and drank their wine. Nestoras remembered songs from long ago, and everyone joined him in his shaky, sweet renditions. Despo's father used to sing these, too. In the midst of all the pleasantness, the pregnant woman's eyelids began to drop.

And then one of the children screamed.

Myrto leapt from her seat. The flames in the

hearth – they must have attacked. As she moved, her skirts whipped them into hissing snakes.

— Enough! Get away from there. Now!

— What happened? asked Agnoulla. Did he burn himself? Careful, child!

The boy whined.

— No!

— Woman! Take him home to bed, yelled Kleanthis, slamming his hand on the table. I've had enough of his stupidity.

— There was a foot!

Another whine.

— What are you talking about?

— There was a foot! In the chimney. It was like the leg of a donkey.

Despo rose from her seat, hand hovering over her stomach. Loukas brought his own hand to hers and stopped, caught somewhere between pushing away her folly and forming a shield.

Myrto narrowed her eyes at her husband.

— What have you been telling him?

Kleanthis broke into a smile, which the wine made liquid.

— It's good for him to learn, he said. To learn what it means to be afraid.

Despo saw the woman, whose husband had been drinking, bite her tongue. Myrto turned and, expelling her own fear, struck the boy's cheek.

— You've made yourself crazy, she said, tucking strands of hair back under her headscarf. You sat too close to the fire and it's made you dizzy. Go sit over there.

The boy moved over to a corner of the room where he sat, whimpering and snivelling, for the rest of the night. After a few minutes Despo went over to check on him, and stroked his arm.

— It's all lies, she said in a soft voice.

But it wasn't the shadows at his back he was watching with naked fear. It was the fireplace, the chimney breast; he was looking out for whatever it was he'd seen inside it, trying to climb into the room.

SECOND DAY OF CHRISTMAS

They went to church to praise the Mother of Christ. For it was Mary who'd been the vessel for His miracle birth, and the catalyst for mankind's salvation. His body was her body, his life her life.

Despo prayed for the Virgin's humanity to pass to her own child. She prayed for him to be born complete and unscathed. She'd been disturbed in the night; having hung a black-handled knife next to the cross behind the door, she'd lowered herself into bed and felt a chill down her spine. With a continuous fire burning in the hearth, the house was as warm as it could be for the winter months. Loukas had brought thorny logs from the woods on Christmas Eve and sprinkled them with nutshells, so the flames were sure to last the next two weeks. But in the cold blue hours she'd been woken by the sound of scurrying feet. It was only foxes or hedgehogs, she'd told herself, but without thinking, she'd grabbed her husband's arm. Loukas was wandering lost in the world of sleep, too far gone to come back quickly. With his eyes closed and his limbs paralysed by slumber, he'd looked as fragile as a baby.

At her side in church, his head was bowed and his eyes were vacant.

He could never save her, just as she could not save him.

*

Loukas crossed himself as he entered the graveyard. There was a fine mist floating between the cypress trees, two hand-widths above the ground and one above the graves. He replaced the beeswax in his father's grave-side lamp and lit it. He prayed for his father's peace in death, and for the forgiveness of his early-departed soul. Panayiotis had been the one to find his body, the day after Christmas, six years ago. Face-down in the creek near the mill, right by the little stone bridge.

Some say his heart failed. Others, that he'd been drinking and stumbled on the stones. Some said, in whispers they thought beyond the reach of Loukas's ears, that something had frightened his father. Everyone knew that unholy beings liked to hide in the places the light couldn't reach, and the danger of them only grew in these days when the waters were unbaptised. But even then Loukas had dismissed the whispers. He knew what it was that had killed his father. It was a sin, and it was thick with shame.

Just a few years beforehand, the British had been recruiting for their army. Loukas's father had stepped forward to join their fight. He'd left the village in his uniform and, less than half a year later, had come back in bandages. They said he'd recovered from his wounds, but Loukas suspected otherwise. Yes, there had been moments when the man's eyes were bright, and he'd been able to regale his visitors with anecdotes for a whole afternoon. He'd tell them about how they'd tied ropes around the donkeys and hoisted them up to the ships for battle. And he'd mimic the braying to make them laugh. For all their theatre, those were the only moments in which Loukas had felt a connection to his father. Outside of them the man was an unknowable master whose voice would rise like a storm when he struck with a leather belt the naked buttocks of his only surviving child. But clarity would give way to fog. The man would sit slumped, staring at nothing, and a fear would whiten his eyes. He'd babble about strange things he saw. They opened his throat, he'd say, gesturing at something behind his son. It seemed there were ghosts in that space, writhing and screaming. They've melted his face, he'd say. And Loukas's mother would brew a pot of sage. His father's tears would run as his cup tipped over, the sage steaming on his thighs. Demons, he'd say. Demons.

By the time his father had returned from fighting, Loukas's mother had also begun to change. Over time she'd got worse. It had started with the loss of feeling in her hands. Then there'd been lesions on her face. She wasn't alone; the village was still not free of the sickness, and they all learned to diagnose it. At last they'd come to take her away, and nobody saw her again. Barely a month later his father had climbed out of bed in the middle of the night and left the house. In the morning, they'd all decided he'd gone to the creek to chase a bandit off his land. But by the will of God, his heart had stopped there.

From within the walls of the cypress trees there came a voice.

— God rest his soul.

Father Michalis, beard sprinkled with grey. He signed the cross over the grave.

— I feel bad, said Loukas. I ought to replace the headstone.

— These things happen, my son. Up here, with the storms and the animals... We'll take care of it in the spring.

Smiling, he placed his hand on the younger man's shoulder. Loukas felt a shiver of guilt, as he always did.

— Come to confession.

— Yes. I will.

— Your father was a good man. But he was suffering, you understand? He never came to speak to me. He should have come.

Loukas kept his eyes on the grave. He couldn't bring himself to raise them.

— Do you understand what I'm saying?

His mouth was too dry, his lips trembled too much to provide an answer. And it was something bilious, the base of something rotten, that he could feel rising up inside him, but he managed to keep it down.

— Yes, he said at last.

After all, was the priest wrong? It was more than a confession his father had needed; it was an exorcism. They ought to have tied him down to the bed and expelled those demons from his head with holy water. They should have shrunk them down to peanuts with the words of the scriptures, kicked them out of the house.

Now look: too late.

*

Despo was shelling black-eyed beans when a knock at the door made her pause. There on the step, where even relatives rarely appeared, stood the Englishman with his wife. She could never remember their foreign names, but she did remember the English for *Good morning* so she used it. They bade her good morning too, in the proper English pronunciation, and thank God at that moment Loukas returned from the vineyard, because what else could she say to them?

The Englishman produced two small packages wrapped in paper, and gave them to Loukas. She heard the English *Thanks* and the Greek words for 'Christmas' and 'orchard'. God have mercy, they

33

were learning! She let out a laugh, but thankfully it was well received. The man and his wife were full of cheer. What fine clothes they wore – you could tell their quality; the wool, the dyes, the gold watches... Not like the rags she tied around her waist and head, the glass beads that dangled at her wrists. Never mind if the Englishwoman was showing her legs like a whore; that's what they did in her country.

A moment later they were gone, and they took the cheer with them. Loukas went to the table, on which he laid the packages carefully before sitting down in his chair to pull off his boots. She saw from the lifted ends of his moustache that he was smiling.

— Are they gifts? she asked.

— Yes. For the work I did in their orchard.

— But they paid you already.

— Make the coffee, woman.

It took her a moment to move. Kindness was not expected of these people. After all, they'd tricked the Turks into taking the island – that was what her father used to say. All well and good, and maybe it had turned out for the best, but she wasn't stupid. No one took land out of goodwill.

While she brewed the coffee, her husband made a ritual of opening the gifts.

— Look at this beauty, he said.

No doubt, it was unusual. The paper had patterns on it in gold leaf like an icon, and the ribbon was made of velvet. The little package was put together better than their entire house. She watched her husband in his worship: a gentle tug at the ribbon, so that it sighed as it slipped away; a lifting of the paper as you would a bridal veil, to reveal a tin box. He opened its lid.

— What is it? she asked, unable to help herself.

— Cake.

— Cake?

It was their English thing, that snowy turd soaked in brandy.

He opened the next parcel, quicker this time. Without the preamble, the next gift came as a shock. There among the sheets of paper lay a pair of woollen socks. Tiny ones. For a child.

Despo crossed herself, and sank into a chair.

— My God. She made those?

Loukas nodded, looking uninterested, and passed them to her.

She stared at the knitted hollow feet in her palm, soon to be filled by her living, breathing son. She'd already made things herself – clothes, socks, a blanket. They sat waiting in a wicker basket by the cot Loukas had built during those weeks in the summer when he'd seemed pleased to have put a child in her. It had curved feet so she could rock it back and forth. How he'd admired his own hand-iwork. How proudly he'd wiped his brow when he'd finished, and how he'd loved showing it off to every visitor.

Why would a stranger do this? She blinked so as not to cry.

Loukas slapped the table.

— Eh! What's happened with the coffee?

She got up to fetch it for him.

*

It was a kind gesture. Loukas gave thanks, so that God would know he was grateful. Christmas cake was a taste he had yet to acquire, but this one had a lightness that was pleasing. That pair of woollen baby socks, on the other hand, had sent a fear rattling through him. They lay loose in their paper wrapper like a snake's shed skin.

God knew Loukas wanted a child. When Despo discovered she was pregnant, she'd been doused in relief. In the beginning he felt the same; that evasion of shame, the satisfaction of success. It was akin to the sense of accomplishment he'd felt on the morning after the wedding, when they'd hung the bedsheets out for the neighbours to see. Or when he'd carried his wife to the house that he and his godfather and cousins had built – men and women having lugged the stones from the river on their backs. And when he'd pulled the head off the rooster to wash the step with its blood.

Kismet, as the Moslems said. He and Despo had been destined to be wed. Parentless youths with little more than a field to their name. The matchmakers would have struggled to find other mates for them. Their godparents had sorted it among themselves, before the kids had had a chance to learn of love or property. Nestoras gifted them a plot of land and helped his godson build on it. The rest was in God's hands.

Loukas gave thanks for Despo. She talked more than any woman should, but she would lay down her life for her loved ones. She even tried, in her girlish way, to divert attention from the annual gloom of his father's death – she who was no stranger to loss. She'd renamed her father's donkey Manolis, so that the beast's name day would fall on this day of St Emmanuel. And as she wished the donkey well on his saint's day, her large smiling eyes would travel to her husband, willing him in on the joy. Instead Loukas would pour, throughout the day, glass after glass of his vineyard's wine, raise each one in a toast to the deceased, then vanish it down his throat. It kept his hand from becoming a fist.

She would make a good mother, he reminded himself.

A light rain had brushed the vineyard; it glistened like a thousand eyes. Loukas put his hands to the leaves the way some men stroked their bloodhounds. Here and there they were sprinkled with flecks of powder. Frost? No. Worse than that. He pruned the infected leaves, praying that the damage stopped there. The past year had been bad enough. God willing, it would not infect the next.

A panic seized him – an illogical thought: he was the cause of this. These lesions on the leaves. Like the splotches he found on his abdomen after waking from certain dreams. No man should dream such things.

If he was sick, then may God cure him. Otherwise, may He have mercy on his soul.

*

The whispering of his name pulled him from the murk of sleep. He opened his eyes to the dark room and the woman in bed beside him. His first thought was that it must be time – Despo's waters had broken.

But no. Even in this blackness he saw her eyes were wide-white, and her moonlit finger was pointing to the window.

— I heard scratching, she said.

She sounded like a little girl, which, thanks to the fog in his head, angered him less than it might have. Before his temper could flourish, he heard it as well: a scratching. As if something was clawing at the house, scrambling to let itself in.

The shadow-woman beside him gasped.

— Go and check, she said. Please. Please.

Loukas hesitated, but it was his duty to protect the souls under his roof. Despo held her stomach, her arms an extra layer over the sheepskin blanket.

Having pulled on his boots and grabbed his rifle, he stepped into the still starlight. Above, the moon was almost full. His breath skittered, cotton-white, ahead of him as he walked. The leaves of the pomegranate tree were shaking, and it took him a moment to realise it wasn't the wind that rattled the bark. A creature was stretched against it. Long, hairy limbs. Loukas fired a shot, startling the thing, which turned to look at him with a sudden flash of its eyes. It sprinted away, its bushy tail sucked into a hedge.

The trunk of the tree was missing a piece, as was a loose pomegranate, its seeds spilling all over the dirt.

THIRD DAY OF CHRISTMAS

The Englishman and his wife had moved into old Spyros's house, God rest his soul. Nobody in the village knew what they had come for, but with any luck they'd found it. It was good to see the place come back to life; the woman seemed to love adorning the windowsills, as well as the courtyard – which you could admire when the front gate was open – with pots of colourful flowers, and the man had cleared away the dirt and rubble from the last quake. The moment man and wife entered the church during the liturgy, the congregation's eyes had turned from the floor, the priest and the icons to the strangers at the door.

William, as they called him, was often seen with a leather-bound book, in which he would write as if catching words in the air and pinning them to the page. From the way he scrutinised the villagers and everything around them, they surmised he was writing about them. Maybe for his King. No one knew what his wife's name was, and if they'd been told, they'd since forgotten. This had been the couple's first Christmas in Cyprus. Judging by the way they bowed their heads to absorb the hymns in

Greek, it appeared they weren't godless. It had been almost six months since their arrival, but the villagers continued to keep their distance from them once the usual friendly greetings had been exchanged. On Christmas Eve, the wife complimented Aliki the Armenian by making satisfied noises at the woven baskets around her doorstep. The old woman, face beaten by hardship, wiped the sweat off her brow with her sleeve and stared. She wished the girl well but continued to watch her, because you never knew where you stood with their kind, until the English couple bade her good day and left.

Thankfully for them, there was at least one local who had taken them to his bosom: the mukhtar. With his usual theatrical air, the man had invited them round to his Christmas feast. He fed them meat and bread and sweets, and gave them wine, and he arranged for a Karagiozis show to be staged for their benefit. The couple sat through the shadow play, not understanding a word of it but smiling in appreciation regardless, wincing only slightly at the volume of the mukhtar's laugh. The man was better fed than most of his subjects, which made him larger, and his laugh louder, like a shout in a cave.

There was a moment of awkwardness when the wife enquired about a woman she'd seen in the village square whose husband had dragged her home by the hair. There was a note of judgement in her soft English voice, but the mukhtar dismissed it – and the episode – as a misunderstanding between cultures. The sea kept countries apart as much as it linked them.

More to his liking was the Englishman, who asked him about the locals, their bloodlines, the roots of their traditions, all for the sake of that book he carried around with him. The mukhtar related what he knew about the Romans, Francs, Venetians, Phoenicians, Saracens – not that he was a scholar of any of these groups. Stories, legends, he knew. Bits he'd been told by parents and grandparents. There were the Turks, of course, of whom thousands remained throughout the towns and villages. A mistake to side with the Germans in the war, and a costly one. But all to the good: Cyprus was better off now, in the King's crown and the Empire's embrace. Most of the mukhtar's knowledge, however, was of the Ancient Greeks, and he specialised in telling the stories of gods and heroes.

The Englishman liked these best. He'd known the tales since childhood, and could scarcely believe he was now on an island where some of the figures he'd read about had lived and died, and then lived again through these tellings. Some of the villagers shared the names of the gods and philosophers in his books: Heracles, Socrates, Aphrodite. He found himself continually dazzled by the chain linking deity to peasant, buried past to present day.

It was this mosaic of history that the Swedes were breaking their backs to unearth. A decent people, on the whole. One of the younger men was especially kind-eyed, which belied his Olympian physique. Fit to pose in an artist's studio, he was, and charmingly bashful. William had struck up a friendship with the overseer, a Dr Lundqvist, a man like the sun: big, round and bright. His white-blonde whiskers bounced with news of progress and discovery, even as he and his colleagues toiled in the August heat – or the sudden, brutal rainstorms of November. So far, the Swedish digs had revealed little more than shards of pottery and stone walls like rows of teeth emerging from the dirt, but the Swedes assured them these were all of immense significance. The old tales had it that these ancient sites and temples served as more than mere churches for pagan worship. The Swede seemed to delight in the Englishman's blushes as he pointed to photographs of profane tablets and pictures of unspeakable acts; to sculptures with exaggerated proportions. The images haunted the Englishman, and had even begun to sneak into his dreams. In the night he felt the warmth of the body next to his, which might once have been strewn on a marble table beneath the burning sun, breast exposed, at the mercy of a copper-skinned Cyprian with a monstrous growth.

William and his wife were here now, for better or worse.

*

At the coffee house, the men toasted Stephanos, Stephanis and Stephos on their shared saint's day. Not in the mood for cheer but longing for the company of men, Loukas sat apart from the shots of zivania and slaps on the back in order to drink by himself in a corner. That was how he was, and everybody had learned to leave him to it.

This time, however, a man pulled up a chair and sat down next to him with a shot of ouzo. Christos. He loomed now; he'd grown into a cypress of a man. His neck alone looked as thick as Loukas's thigh.

— What's new, friend? said Christos, but his expression showed no friendship – his eyes were like a wolf's.

— Same old.

— When's your wife going to drop?

— How should I know?

— Easy! I only asked a question.

The other man looked amused by Loukas's silence.

— I'm talking to you like a friend. Why are you so sour?

Loukas wouldn't meet his eye. The two men did, at one point, have something approaching a friendship. As boys they would bathe in the creek together and hunt for songbirds. But that was long before the marriage to Despo. Ever since, Christos spat on the street when he caught sight of man or wife. Loukas's palms were damp. He despised altercations, had avoided them throughout his life. But he couldn't help clenching his fists. He held his breath. The fight was brewing; you could feel it in the air the way cats could feel a coming snowfall. Then Christos got up, thumping the table. The motion made the smaller man flinch, which only made the other laugh. Christos looked him up and down, spat on the floor and walked to another table. Loukas took a sip of his coffee.

After that a couple of others came in and greeted the room.

— Afternoon, Loukas! said one of them, Anthis, after spotting him in the corner. When's the baby coming?

— God only knows, my friend.

Christos looked up.

— Let me buy you a drink now, we can celebrate again later, said Anthis.

— Well, if you're buying...

— Are you going to stay sitting over there? How are we going to chat?

— I'm comfortable now. And don't worry, they can hear you in Paphos.

Anthis cackled and turned back to his friends. Loukas tried to retain a smile on his face, while thinking how much he wanted to be alone, just as he always did. From when he was a boy he'd liked to sit in the fields, hidden in the tall yellow grass, or sneak into the neighbour's stables to commune wordlessly with the horses. Christos had noticed this trait in him and teased him about it. You'll become a monk, he'd said one day when they were boys. Loukas had taken offence at this, and struck his friend in the chest. The tussle had turned bitter, Loukas digging his nails into Christos's face, and Christos grabbing him between the legs and twisting. Though they'd got over their spat, it occurred to Loukas now that the episode was the beginning of the end of their friendship.

The men were laughing at something. From what he snatched of the conversation, Loukas understood it was to do with the Other Folk. Stephanos was joking about staying indoors after dark, lest he found himself suddenly with child.

— It's been known to happen, said one with a wink.

— You'll have little demon offspring.

— Even uglier than you are.

— Big man like me, I know how to deal with a kalikantzaro.

— It's the English I'm talking about!

Laughter, drink, more laughter. They carried on down this road, one minute trying to chill each other's bones with stories they'd heard of the tricksters and gold cups of wine revealed to be hooves of piss, and the next minute waving the nonsense away.

How separate the Englishman William was to them, a different being entirely. What must he think

49

of them, the peasants, with barely a scrap of cloth between them, their teeth black with rot? How Despo's bread-loaf arms compared to the Englishwoman's fiddlesticks. How William's leather shoes glinted next to the dull mud of Loukas's boots. The sight of the Englishman in church that morning, with his pretty wife in a strange hat, had only made his oddness clearer. At times Loukas wished he could speak English. From their few interactions in the orchards, built on mime and learned phrases, and from observing the man's brilliant smile and his quiet focus as he wrote – not only wrote, but at great speed – in his leather-bound book, or the way he reached for the machine in his pocket to take pictures of this fruit and that gate, this miner and that farmhand, Loukas had the notion he was more akin to the outsider than these others. These others, who roared at dirty jokes and threw chairs across rooms when the joke turned out to be them. Of course, Loukas squashed these thoughts. No one hated the English as they had their former rulers, but you weren't going to make one of them your best man, either.

A couple of tables away, Christos was losing a backgammon game to Mehmet. His temper had begun to flare more often since the Greeks were thrown out of Turkey, and it usually erupted at Mehmet. Christos got up, stretching to his full length, chest high, and he stabbed the board with his finger.

— How in the hell does a man get so many doubles?

— Mashallah! Stephanos said to Mehmet with a chuckle, which only stoked the fire in Christos.

The big man lunged at the seated one. Stephanos grabbed him by the sleeve. Christos then turned on him, for the damage to his shirt. They all yelled at each other. Stephanos held Christos's shirt and Christos held his, both of them stretching towards each other, faces a finger apart, but before any punches were thrown and before he was asked to leave, Christos made his exit, cursing the Turk for his underhand ways. Mehmet shook his head in disbelief, smiling. And as he left, Christos shot a look at Loukas, as if he longed to punch him, too.

FOURTH DAY OF
CHRISTMAS

It was the midwife's name day, so when she came to check on Despo she brought with her a plate of kourabiedes.

— Many happy returns, said the younger woman, looking more like a child by the day, as she pushed herself up from the chair.

— Girl! Sit down right now. Eat.

So Despo stuffed the sweet in her mouth. The sugar-powder left a white cloud on her lips.

— Ah, so they turned out good. I can see it in your face.

— Yours are the best, said the pregnant one with a moan. No question. Bless your hands.

If there was something you wanted to know about baking, you asked Domna. She got her talent from her dear departed mother, who had also delivered children. Midwifery ran in those women's blood. Despo wondered if Domna, though she had given her husband five sons about whom she often gloated, was perhaps a little heartbroken to be the last of the line.

— So, what does the baby say? asked the midwife. Is he ready to come out?

— You tell me.

— Leave him where he is, you look all right.

— That's what I think. Everyone's rushing me. I don't want him to come now, anyway.

— What are you talking about?

Despo licked her fingers clean. She shifted in her seat, to mask her discomfort.

— Better after Epiphany.

The older woman gave her a look. In the sunlight poking through the parted curtains, her pretty green eyes were like a cat's. She smiled.

— Yes, that's right, she said.

— I think Loukas would rather he never came at all.

Despo hadn't meant to say it aloud. God help her, why could she never stop herself from talking?

Thankfully, the midwife only shrugged.

— That's what they're all like, love. They'd kill us for saying it, but men are scared of being fathers. Because they know they'll be useless at it. He's shitting himself now, but he'll be fine once he sees the baby.

— I hope so, said Despo, her discomfort blooming.

As she turned the shortbread in her mouth, she played with the words she wished to get off her chest, and the order in which to speak them.

— Tell me, said the midwife.

— I wake up in the middle of the night.

— To piss?

— That's nothing new. I mean, I hear things that wake me up.

— It's your dreams, my love. It's common. Soulla had nightmares for three months straight.

— What did she do?

— We took the fear out of her. We took her out to the orchard, she jumped over the fire and she forgot about it. Finished.

Despo had seen this done before, to her mother. She had never connected it to one of the pregnancies. How she wished she'd understood back then. But the years had fallen away like ears of corn; people and their lives turned to dust. At least nothing was troubling her mother now, God rest her soul.

The midwife took a huge breath.

— Come, she said, let's look you over.

Despo steadied herself on the table as Domna helped her up. When she looked down at her puffy hands, she realised with a start that one of her fingernails had split.

*

The man they called William had decided to walk through the woods with his book. It wasn't solely the people he was writing about, but also the plants and trees and birds, the beasts and serpents, the island itself. The mukhtar had told him of the mouflon, which still slunk about the pines and cedars of Cyprian woodland, but the man had warned him he'd be lucky to see it. For this reason alone the Englishman had his camera to hand. So far, he'd used it to document the women feeding loaves to the ovens in the square, and the brown-skinned farmers bent over their work in the fields.

On the ground before him was the trunk of a tree, felled by the recent thunderstorms. For whatever reason, the sight of it brought a lump to his throat and he started to cry. Perhaps he missed his people. Wiping his eyes, he resumed his walk and followed the sound of running water. In time it brought him to the creek near the mill. There, where a stone bridge built by one of the invaders arced, placid as a caterpillar, he bent down to the water and brought a palmful to his mouth. Its freshness made him gasp.

Rustling. Scratching.

The man looked about him, and from the midst of the foliage a form appeared. A brown head, a white mouth. Horns, somewhere between ribbed and scaled, curved like the handles of an amphora. The creature stared at him in silence, then in the space of a single breath it was swallowed back into the woods.

The Englishman cursed himself. Instead of taking its picture, he'd simply gawked like a fool. But how fortunate he had been. How slim the chance. A mouflon! He could scarce believe it, and laughed, aloud and to himself, at the sight he had been so blessed to witness. It felt like a portent. He returned his hands to the fresh water of the creek and brought it to his face. Along with the unexpected coldness in the air, it gave him a pleasing jolt. Almost mindlessly, he found himself lowering his head to it, to drink directly from the stream as an animal might. The act brought on a sensation so thrilling he didn't dare contemplate it further. He raised himself.

And then he beheld another sight, one that made his hand go straight to his heart, almost dropping the camera. A figure, thin, dark, hairy, was coming towards him. Skittish, purposeful. It was only as it got close that the bulging eyes relaxed and warmed, and the creature's face became familiar: Loukas.

Taken aback by the man's odd behaviour, the Englishman made a point of looking relieved and jovial as he said a *hullo* and asked what was the matter. With his minimal English there was no way the peasant could respond. He only gestured at the water, then at the Englishman, and finally he wiped his brow to express a journey from concern to relief. The men paused and went silent. They understood each other, which made even this small moment feel significant. It was a joining; an imminent closeness.

Though not grotesque, the women of Aphrodite's island were somewhat lacking. Yet the men, with their work-strong physiques, black eyes and copper skin, were constantly startling. Loukas was a slenderer

59

specimen, and was separated further from the others by a rather becoming air of melancholy. He sat silent as others shouted. He excavated with his eyes what others only glanced at. And when he pruned the orchards, his hands were as soft on the branches, and on the hanging fruit, as a spring breeze. His was a comforting presence, a captivating darkness.

The Englishman put his arm on the Cyprian's shoulder, and the Cyprian in turn placed his hand on his back. A sense of alarm began to rise; they felt it between them, both of them, and all through the trees. It rang out like the cry of a bird. As if guided by an invisible other hand, the Englishman touched that melancholy Cyprian face and then, as if similarly guided, the face moved closer to him. Their lips came together.

The men pulled themselves apart and stared at each other, as if each had caused offence. They stood defiant, like brawlers in the coffee house, like stags. Their breaths intertwined. An odd sensation took each man's head; he felt a shift, a movement from one plane of existence to another. He saw his hand grab hold of the other's shirt. One man saw black hairs on a foreign chest; the other saw the fairness of immigrant skin, saw it pulsing and felt his own heart pulsing, the blood that pumped remorseless. Together they fell to the ground, or one pushed the other down, head thumping against the felled tree.

At the Englishman's palms was hairy flesh, and at his face was a pair of bold black eyes, at his mouth a heat thus far unknown to him, and against his leg, against his stomach, a touch that brought to mind the photographs of primitive sculptures, their potent limbs, and the sordid goings-on in temples beneath the glare of the sun and the gods.

*

Man and wife ate their soup in silence.

Despo longed to tell Loukas of the midwife's visit. Their boy would be healthy, and she was progressing just right. She longed to share the visions that disturbed her sleep, her constant aches, her morning sickness, and to entertain him with the funny anecdotes Domna had shared of pregnancies, births and the antics of her own children when they were toddlers. The knowledge that all this suffering would be worth it if their boy came out breathing and carried on doing so. But it – all of it, whether good or bad – would only incite Loukas's anger, or at least his sullenness. For once in her life, she ought to shut up.

— Are you feeling well? she heard herself asking.

Loukas looked up, alarmed.

— Why?

She placed the back of her hand against his cheek.

— Your face is burning.

He moved his head. For a long time, he sat looking into his bowl as if he might read his future

61

in it. A downturned head tells you nothing. And never did a curling lock of hair so resist another's touch. Why could he not just let her love him?

Overcome by an unfamiliar heat, her hand balled into a fist. She felt, for the first time in their marriage, on the edge of a reckless act; a fist slammed down on the table, a yell in her throat. It took her back to her youth on the farm, climbing onto the stables and teetering over the edge in the knowledge that a single movement in the wrong direction could change the course of her life.

— I'll make some tea, she said instead, and got up from the table.

Nothing from Loukas.

Despo shut her eyes and let the breath pour out of her body, in one long stream till she felt faint.

She'd done it again. She had made her husband retreat into his body, like a turtle in danger. Any more of this and all she'd be left with was a shell.

FIFTH DAY OF
CHRISTMAS

When Loukas's father returned from the war, the English gave him a medal. After his mother had shed tears of pride, the question remained: what were they supposed to do with it? There was nowhere in the house to display a medal, so she hung it from the crucifix nailed to the door. Loukas had grown used to the sight of the shining metal disc at Jesus's bleeding feet, and the pictures embossed upon it. On the front was the head of the King of England, mostly in shadow, but you knew from his expression he was calm and wise. Around him, a halo of unknown symbols. English letters. And on the back of the medal, a fantasy scene: a naked man riding his horse. Loukas's mother would go red in the face when as a child he would laugh and point at the naked man. As he grew up, the medal caught his eye more often. The King's neatly trimmed beard on one side, and on the other an unknown muscular soldier astride a fearsome beast – hanging sword, swooping calf, a confident grip on the horse's reins, all the lines on the nude man's body expressing ease and masculine power. Loukas saw the image in his dreams. The man strode over fields littered with corpses, pulsing with life himself. A god among the graves. And Loukas, young, confused, would wake with jolts of fear and shame. In his adult life, he had managed to keep the dreams, those abominable images, at bay. He had married Despo, he had consummated their union, he had hung the bloodstained sheets outside the house he'd built. He was a man like any other. And in confession he'd wished blandly to be forgiven of sin, just like everyone else.

Then the Englishman came. Hair like a flame, eyes like ice.

The mukhtar had brought them together. He was the one who, when the foreigner sought a pair of hands to tend his orchards, directed William to the quiet winemaker. On the one hand, Loukas had been hesitant to accept the duty for fear of what others might say, not to mention a wariness of the English themselves. But on the other he was in need of the extra income. And he didn't have much to do with the strangers. The man would sometimes come to check on him – with suspicion, Loukas thought at first, before realising that the Englishman might be lonely and eager to practise some of the Greek he'd learned. He would point at a quince and Loukas would say the word. The man would repeat it, smiling though squinting and perspiring in the sun.

What happened… no, it didn't happen. It was a lie, a trick. Satan was working through this man, using him. He was casting spells with one of his demons. Loukas's own dormant filth was being flung at him, to confuse, to scare, to shame and destroy him. Or it was being deployed to test him. The Englishman was a trial from God. With his creamy skin he came to offer a forbidden taste and Loukas, the idiot, had taken the bait.

In the vineyard he beheld the proof of his sin. With sorrow and fury, he pruned the leaves that were splotched with white. Disease. That's what this was: a reminder. What it stirred in him, disease. The memory of breath at his ear, disease. The grip on his chest, on his throat, on his tongue, disease.

He could not afford to be infected. It would destroy not only the next year's crop, but also Loukas himself, his home.

Despo.

Their unborn child.

He dusted the vines with sulphur and prayed for God's mercy.

*

Despo went to visit Aliki, because the old woman's Christmas wasn't for another week and she might be feeling adrift. Outside the house, she was greeted by every passing neighbour. But across the road lived Christos, and he stood huge in the darkness beneath the wooden balcony. She was about to bid him good morning, but something in his glare warned her not to provoke him. He brought to mind the local butcher's dogs, which leapt to gnash and growl in a rage the moment you set eyes on them. Christos spat on the ground. She felt a flush of anger, which pleased her, since it masked her dread. She turned her face to Aliki's door and knocked.

Only God knew what that man had against her. As children they'd spent many a happy hour playing by the carob trees, whacking each other with the pods in an imagined swordfight. He and her husband even shared a godfather. It occurred to her he might have put the Eye on them. That would explain the lumps and dips of the preceding year.

No sooner had she touched the Evil Eye on her bracelet than, thankfully, the Armenian's door opened. Aliki came out to kiss her on both cheeks.

Along with a basket of vines, Despo had brought a dish of paximadia so they could dip them in their coffees. Aliki thanked her with more kisses and blessings, and brought out her jars of spoon sweets.

— Melon or cherry?

— Whatever you want.

— It's not whatever I want, it's whatever you want, my love. We don't want the baby getting marks.

Despo loved melon and cherry equally. She chose melon, because it reminded her of summer, and besides, it would satisfy the woman. But she was slow to eat the sweet. Her teeth and gums ached, and the crunch of the candied peel made her wince.

Both women picked up the vines and started to weave. It was a habit Despo had slipped into over the past year. The Armenian was getting old, and unable to keep to her former pace. But her pride blinded her to her performance. Even the dwindling coins in her purse didn't wake her up. At first Despo used the excuse of wanting to learn, so she could weave the baskets to carry her husband's wines and vinegars to markets and fairs. Over the months she slept a little easier for having contributed, even in this small way, to the old woman's security. If it wasn't for Loukas, she would have brought Aliki into their home as soon as they'd moved in.

— Does your back hurt? Aliki asked, because the younger woman was wriggling on the straw chair.

— Oof, all the time.

— I had that, too, for all of mine. And the sickness, oh my God...

— I don't get that so much.

— You're lucky.

The younger woman kissed her cross.

— I'm making the powder soon, said Aliki.

— Ah, thank you.

— I would make him some clothes, but... my eyes aren't so good anymore.

— Bless you. But don't worry, there's no need. The English came round the other day. The wife made socks, can you believe it? She gave them to us as a gift.

— You don't say!

— I swear. Looks like the English have souls, too.

— Eh, I'll say a prayer for them as well, then.

They laughed, and drank their coffees.

— I've lived a thousand lives, said the Armenian. I've known a thousand people. I've loved them, I've buried them. The Turks killed my whole family – they wiped out all our neighbours and friends. You think I'm going to hate Esme because of it? What did she ever do to me? Fatima and her kids? What did they ever do? We all bleed. We all suffer, and we all die. Whatever we call our God and however we worship Him, we're all the same. The English are just us with other tongues. They're people too.

She finished her coffee and grinned.

— Even if they look like vampires.

*

When he left the vineyard Loukas made straight for the coffee house. On the way there, by the bare almond tree, Hassan's daughter was tickling a dog and laughing as it both surrendered to pleasure and barked its complaints. On seeing her, it entered Loukas's mind that he did like children – they were sweet when they were good – and so he greeted her

warmly. She flinched and turned her face from him.
She was wrapped against the cold, and it hid her well.

— What's wrong with you? Don't you know me?

The girl, after a moment's reflection, nodded.

— So what's with you?

— Did you kill someone? she asked.

He was bemused. But she looked nervous, and
deadly serious.

— What are you talking about?

— Yesterday, at the creek. I saw you hit someone
and fall down. I ran away.

A punch in the heart. His whole body stopped.

— What else did you see?

He could hear the tremor in his own voice.

— Are you Loukas?

— Of course I am.

— Show me your leg.

— Aishe, what did you see?

— I heard a weird language. It wasn't your voice.
Then something grabbed you and you threw it on
the ground.

Loukas's head felt light. He spoke as if through
another's skull.

— Yes, that's what happened. I fought someone.

— A kalikantzaro? The girl was looking at him,
eyes wide as coffee cups.

— Who told you about them?

She didn't answer.

On the inside, he prayed to God. On the outside, he nodded.

— Yes, he said. But don't worry. They only attack us Christians.

— That's not what the others say.

— Who?

She named some of the older boys.

— They're just trying to scare you. Don't listen to them.

She didn't answer, only carried on looking at his legs.

He carried on to the coffee house. Let her believe the nonsense. It would do the child good to learn fear, to pause before venturing out alone in the dark or to speak to people she didn't know. If fear took the form of a dirty, crooked, hairy creature, then so be it. He looked back at her and saw that she was staring at him, frozen with alarm. Mashallah.

The coffee house was full and the men already yelling when Loukas arrived. It wasn't much of a place, but Pantelis served the best loukoumia in the village to go with the zivania. Your teeth sank into the sweets as if into flesh, and their luminous rose or citrus bodies, dusted with sugar, always made Loukas think of buried jewels. As usual, the backgammon sets were splayed open on the tables. And hovering over one of them was Christos, thick as a boar and tossing his amber worry-beads along the range of his fingers as if he owned everyone in the room, as if he was the mukhtar.

Loukas almost turned around to leave. But he stopped himself and, with an air of indifference, went to take a seat in the corner.

— Come, play me, said Christos.

— I didn't come to play.

— I'll play, said old Yiorkis. Let me steal back some of what you stole from me last time.

Nobody took the old man seriously; he always had that smile on his face – as if his head had been caught in the olive press.

— I was talking to Loukas.

Christos was eyeing him with a smirk, one hand on his knee.

— You afraid of me? Christos asked him.

— What would I be afraid of?

— So sit.

Loukas sat down at Christos's table. Why would the other man antagonise him? Perhaps Loukas had misread him this past year. Perhaps the other man's snipes and sneers were in his head.

Pantelis brought over booze and loukoumia. Loukas took a sip of the drink. The sweets on the plate he tried to ignore. Their peachy hue and the powdered sugar now reminded him of what they shouldn't.

He needn't have suppressed the thought, though, because Christos brought him up.

— I hear you're tending his orchards. The Englishman.

His die rolled and slapped the edge of the board.

— For some time now. And?

— Are you friends?

Christos got the higher number, so he went first.

— White.

He moved his chips. Five, three.

— So, are you friends?

— What, with an Englishman? You think I suddenly learned another language, to become friends with him?

He rolled a double. Four moves.

Christos threw his fist on the table. Once the chips stopped trembling, there was no other sound.

— What do you think they're here for? Halloumi pie? You think they're going to set us free and go?

The man talked, and the dice rolled, and the chips moved along and off the board, and the other men watched and smoked, and the coffee cups and bottles clinked and rattled on the tables, and the wind rattled the bones of trees outside in the twilight, and all the while Loukas went inside his head, where William was waiting. He saw the fire and ice. He saw the pleasure and pain. He even felt it, though he tried not to, not while this other man was breaking him up to absorb him. He felt a pulsing in his heart, which travelled to the veins in his arms, to the hand that clenched and moved the chips along and off the board.

Christos's words had been interrupted by some of the others, who either chipped in with agreements or contradicted him entirely. Loukas spoke, purely so as to have a voice.

— Am I the one who invited the English for dinner? Go speak to the mukhtar – what have I got to do with anything?

Christos rolled his dice and moved his chips almost without taking his eyes off Loukas.

— I've heard you with him. *Merry Christmas!* he added in English, with the high voice of a girl.

He'd barely noticed that Loukas was winning.

— *Merry Christmas*, said Loukas, finishing the game.

The surprise kept Christos mute for a minute, maybe more. Everyone was watching them. Then he stood up to his full height, so big his head almost touched the dried gourds that hung from the beams, and with a flip of his hand he turned the board upside down and onto the floor, where the chips shot off in all directions.

Heart pounding, hairline damp, but retaining his composure, Loukas put the whole loukoumi into his mouth and licked his fingers clean of the sugar.

*

It was a noise, either from within her dream or outside the window, that woke Despo in the pitch black.

But she soon forgot it when she became aware of her unsettled bowels. Without another thought she got out of bed, trying not to move too quickly because of her condition. And yet she had to rush, before it was too late. As she went for the door she felt that flutter in her stomach, the signal for the imminent near-liquid she'd started to shit on a regular basis this past week. In the darkness she saw the wooden cross and the black-handled knife behind the door. She stopped. Was that movement she could hear? Rustling, crunching. She put her ear to the door and listened. One breath in, one breath out, and outside, the breath of late December. Nothing else. She creaked the door open and looked around first. Then she stepped out.

Once outside, she couldn't move fast enough. Her own feet rustling and crunching, dead twigs, snail shells, she made her way to the outhouse. It occurred to her the ground was dry. Loukas had been complaining of the constant rains of late, how damaging they'd be for the vines. She'd suggested making koupepia from the leaves so they'd at least have food on the table, if not a decent product from the grapes. Her husband had looked at her as if she'd spat on the cross.

It was black in the outhouse, but she knew how to get in position to aim for the hole. A childish fear made her look back at the pit in case of snakes, but all she saw was a blot of ink. It was winter, the snakes would be hiding. Over the past few weeks it had become yet more of a challenge to lower herself. So she did what had become her new norm: bend her knees while spreading her palms on opposite walls of the wooden box.

A flip in her belly. Her heart lurched. For a panicked second she thought the baby might fall out now, into this filthy pit. It was crazy, but she had heard of it happening; mothers giving birth while standing up. They'd be cleaning the kitchen and out the baby would come. But these tended to be older women, whose bodies were practised in delivering fresh pairs of hands for the land and loom. Her labour would be her first, and it would be agony. A different agony to this.

She prayed for a healthy baby. She prayed for a happy husband, and a good year.

She was frozen, and now so was the movement in her bowels. The flutter turned to stone. She looked back again at the black pit.

The Arabs of the village spoke of jinn, demons that hid in dark and dirty places. So many different people spoke of evil beings, all of them alike in vital ways.

It's all lies.

Had she said that aloud?

No sooner had the words come than she heard a noise. Scratching. It was scratching she could hear, between the whistles of the wind. Her heart pattered as she moved her eyes from hinge to hinge on the door of the outhouse, from the nails that held the walls together to the gaps between wood and earth.

The noise – all noise – was replaced by a ringing in her ears. She realised she wasn't breathing.

Rustling.

One of those things was out there. Eating worms or snails. She could hear the crunch of the shell. Good Folk. Her father had said to call them the Good Folk.

And then it came to her: she pulled at a loose string on her shift, snapped it, and held it tight. The coldness had left her. So had the ringing in her ears. She opened the door of the outhouse and stepped outside, crossing the air with her two fingers like a priest. Nothing. There'd be nothing. It was all lies. She'd go back inside where her husband's sleeping body was waiting with its warmth, with its sad half-smile.

But there by the pomegranate tree, in the dim white light of the moon, was a black figure. It came towards her, and she walked up to it with the string in her hand, air sweeping up her nape, arms tingling, other hand on her stomach. Then the creature spoke her name, making her gasp.

— Loukas!

— What is it? What's wrong?

He was here. She'd been calling for him, the sound had escaped her, but here he was. Her husband.

— What's happened? What's wrong with you?

And she was clinging to his shirt. Her real, actual husband. The earth and vine of his scent. Her arms clasped his warmth as his body slowly moved its limbs to hold her back. She loved her husband. Thank God for Loukas. Thank God.

SIXTH DAY OF
CHRISTMAS

The girl Aishe had gone and told her father what Loukas had done by the creek. Hassan came knocking on the door as Loukas was dipping a paximadi in his coffee. Loukas turned to see his wife's hand go up to block the man as he barged into the house.

— What's this shit you've been saying to my child?

— Hassan, please, said Despo. Calm down.

— Woman, said Loukas, warning her.

Despo backed away, and watched as Hassan approached her husband, looking intent on battering his brains in.

— She won't even sleep now, she's so scared about what you told her.

— What did you tell her? asked Despo.

— Quiet, woman! said Loukas.

— Telling her about demons in the woods, about how they're the children who died unbaptised, that they stink of sweat and piss and they want to torture you, and they've got the legs of goats and who knows what other nonsense.

— Hassan, you have my word: I didn't say any of that to her. She heard it all from others, probably Anthis's boys.

— Bullshit.

— It's the time of year – they hear it from their parents and they tell each other.

— She said she saw you with one in the woods. You. Why would she mention you?

Loukas couldn't help a glance at Despo. Her confusion brought a flush to his cheeks. Thoughts flicked through his mind like a deck of cards; images and symbols fanned out in random order.

— She saw me in the woods, he said at last. I was arguing with Christos. He started again in the coffee house later, ask anyone. The rest of it she dreamt up. She's a child, Hassan.

— Yes, she's a child. And you told her you fought a goblin.

— She asked me. As if she wanted to hear a story. I said yes, I thought it was what she wanted to hear. I swear, I didn't mean to scare her. I thought she wanted a story. I didn't mean to scare her.

— Eh...

— You have my word, my friend. Come, sit. Have a coffee with us.

By the time the Turk left their house he was contented. Despo had wrapped some paximadia in cloth for him to take to his wife and children.

What else did she have? They were all as poor as each other.

With company gone, the house was filled with the silence of their marriage. Despo stole a glance at Loukas as she moved around the table to begin on the lentils. What could you tell about a man from the back of his head? What would she see if she could open it up like a pod of pulses? But she wanted to. Yes, now, more than ever, she wanted him to open himself up. To reveal what he thought, what he kept to himself, what he had seen in the woods. But for once she kept her silence. From now on she would think of nothing but peace.

But her head would not allow it. In her mind was Loukas's voice telling her to shut up. A different voice from the one that assuaged Hassan, as if belonging to another being. When had he last spoken to her with such gentleness? Had he ever in their marriage? Here she was, in constant pain, without so much as a caress.

Her husband surprised her by speaking.

— She saw nothing.

Despo allowed his words to repeat in her head, and felt her arms go rigid.

— She's a child. She was dreaming. It's all rubbish.

Loukas's boot kicked against the chair as he got up, startling her. He came back a moment later with a bottle of their wine. He took a cup and, sitting back down, poured himself a drink and threw the liquid down his gullet.

Despo heard only the sound of his breath, uneven, shaky. He had left the cupboard door open, and inside she saw the folded cloth in which her torn fingernail sat, waiting for Epiphany.

*

By the afternoon it seemed as if everyone had heard of Loukas's encounter with the goblin in the woods. Girls in shawls, breaking rocks into pebbles for the new roads; men lugging sacks thrown over their shoulders; all stopped him to ask about it, some with rounded eyes and others with crooked smiles. Hambis, with a tray of fresh bread balanced on one shoulder and a folding chair resting on the other, gave him a wink.

— Careful you don't end up with two kids now!

For a moment Loukas was too stunned to reply. If Hambis meant that Despo's womb was infected by demon seed, he ought to cross himself against it. But if the neighbour was implying something else, Loukas ought to straighten his back, puff out his chest, dare him to repeat his accusation like a man. Instead, he gave the same response as he had to the others: he'd made it up, he'd told the girl a tale. But it was clear from numerous pairs of eyes that the doubt was already settling in.

His name, in the air. Father Michalis was calling to him from across the street. Loukas stood still, watching the black cassock float towards him in the quiet light. The day of St Joseph was a blessedly dry one, alone amid the rains that soaked the vines.

— My son, I've heard your news. You saw one of the creatures.

— No, Father, you've heard wrong.

— But Fatima said you told her daughter...

— I told the girl a story.

— She saw something. She saw you and something else by the creek.

— Yes...

— Christos denies it.

Loukas felt fingertips run along his spine.

— Christos?

— Yes. Some of the gossips were saying it was him you were fighting in the woods. He said it was nonsense.

Loukas nodded.

— Yes, nonsense.

Father Michalis placed his hand on the young man's shoulder and steered him towards the shadow of the stairs leading up to Eleni the weaver's house. From here they had a view of the English couple's residence, Spyros's old place. And it was at this moment that the Englishman, for the first time since the incident in the woods, showed his face in the village. He mounted the bicycle that spent most of the day drowsing against the outer wall of the house, and he went off without so much as a glance in the others' direction. Loukas watched those legs, in their crisp, pale trousers, work the machine.

— How is Despo doing? asked the priest.

— Fine. Fine.

— Is she sleeping?

— So-so. She gets up in the night.

— Watch her. Always keep her in your sights now. We don't know how these beings will attack. How they might infect.

— Father...

— We both know it wasn't Christos.

— No. It wasn't Christos.

To admit this was a light relief, like the lukewarm light that day.

— You must protect her – do whatever is necessary now that the baby is close.

— Thank you, Father, but I don't want to scare her. She's already afraid.

— And she'll be more afraid if you don't do your duty.

— Yes, Father.

The priest squeezed his shoulder.

— You're a good lad. But there's a lot inside you. You don't have to carry it alone. Come to confession, rid yourself of the burden.

He indicated his own heart.

— God is here.

Yes, God was there, but so was the Devil. And among Mary and the angels sat the demons and goblins. In Loukas's heart the Virgin's face was a quilt of lesions, and she suckled a beast with cloven hooves. The Devil had round blue eyes and a fair moustache. He cast the ghosts of long-dead men in corners of rooms to make a head go weak, to spill sage on withered legs. And he burrowed inside Loukas. He was bewitching. Beautiful and clawed as a siren.

*

In the cellar Loukas felt the darkness closing in on him. He tried to focus his thoughts on the task at hand: the wine on which the household relied – the only thing his father had had to pass on. The liquid poured clear from the tap into the cask, but the taste... Sour. He tried it again. Without a doubt, sour. Perhaps it was him. The sickness had coloured his sense of taste. He felt a swell of sadness that clogged his throat and pushed tears to his eyes. He shook his head, in the way dogs did. He steadied himself against a barrel and took a few deep breaths. Then he went to the stairs to call for Despo, who came down the stairs to sample it, too.

— It's fine, she said of the taste.

He could tell she was lying.

— It's fine. It's good.

She was trying to please him. Between them was her belly, its very own being now that her labour was fast approaching. He flinched when her stomach moved nearer to him – in this dark room, where his filth was quickly gathering. He ordered her to go upstairs and take a bath in the light.

— Loukas, what did you see in the woods?

The question startled him. He opened his mouth to speak but nothing came.

— Tell me.

She watched him, as a cat in a hedge might watch a stranger.

He couldn't tell her. How could he? He choked back his tears and held her face as gently as he could.

— Go upstairs and have a bath, he said, in what he hoped was a softer voice.

But she felt the trembling of his fingers, and it passed to her lips.

— You're afraid.

They were her words, not his.

But she did as she was told, because she wanted to. She prepared a bath in the light of the blue afternoon, and she sprinkled it with olive leaves. She wore her wooden cross in the water, held it at her chest. The pregnancy had begun as a relief and a joy. But it had left her impaired, with these ghastly veins and the constant aches. It kept her tired and weak, flitting between constipation and diarrhoea. She'd been unable to bend, to clean the place more thoroughly, now when they needed cleanliness most. Her stitching and sewing had become a trial, her pace more than halved. How much she would have to make up for once the baby was here. How much she would do to right the imbalance. Loukas would not have to worry about profits from the wine; after all, he was right, it was a little sour. Already the coming year was bleak.

God would see them through. She prayed. Held by the water, cleansed and soothed, she felt herself go light. As tenderly as a snowflake settling on a branch, a thought came to her: what if there was something wrong with Loukas, something at his core, deeper than she knew? After all, the wine was no good. The vines were diseased. Something had happened in the woods, something he wouldn't speak of, there by the unbaptised waters. And it wasn't another woman, of that she was certain. Loukas, despite his tender face, despite the warmth of his rare smile, was not that sort of man. Nor was he the man she thought she'd known. He was sullen, dazed, angry, absent – now, when he should have been at his happiest. As if his were the body being changed.

He appeared in the corner of her eye. She turned to him, this man, whoever he was, looking gloomily at her. Her hand tightened its grip on the wooden cross. She could have sworn it made him wince. The water stuffed her ears like wax. It filled her head so that she floated and sank at the same time. She lifted herself out of the bath as her husband removed his clothes. The coarse black hair on that soft skin when he rid himself of shirt and undershirt; the cobbles of his spine rising to a mountain range as he took off his boots; the thin legs with their strong calves, exposed as he unravelled the vraka from them; all of him was at once both known and foreign.

She stood back to dry herself and observe him. He lowered himself into the bath, shadows over his face, the dangling dark between his legs, and he groaned, suppressing something at the same time as unleashing it, a bigger sound, an anguish, and at last he was immersed in the water sprinkled with olive leaves.

Hanging from the door, next to the cross, was the black-handled knife. Its blade caught the light. She could use it, if she had to. In any case, if something had got into Loukas she was as good as widowed.

In the evening they would go to vespers, and she would pray for them all to defeat this.

*

There was another tale she'd heard. One about a girl in the village who loaded a donkey with wheat to take to the mill, because her mother had fallen sick. The woman, in her weakened state, warned her daughter not to go. But the girl insisted. When she got to the mill night had fallen, and the air was filled with the sound of fiddles and laughter. Assuming the presence of fellow villagers, she went inside. But what she found made her gasp. It wasn't humans in the mill but five of the other beings. They were hopping around on their donkey legs, long tongues and long ears wagging. Then they turned their bold red eyes on her. She backed away but they pounced; her heart went into her mouth, and they dragged her further in.

Come in, my beauty.

Where are you going?

We've been waiting a while for a beautiful girl.

Come and dance with us.

— Of course I want to dance with you, said the girl, mustering all the calm she could manage. But first I must grind this wheat.

And before they answered back, she threw the wheat onto the millstone and began to grind.

Dance with us and we'll give you gifts. Silk dresses, golden jewels, velvet slippers, barrels of goods for your dowry!

— Very well, she said. Go and fetch those things while I do this, and then I promise I'll dance with you till dawn.

The creatures ran off, cackling.

The girl's heart beat faster and faster as wheat was turned to flour, and she prayed for the work to be done in time. When she had finished, she loaded the baskets onto the donkey and off she went home, the laughter of the Other Folk echoing from beyond the pines as she went.

Back home, she fell into her mother's embrace.

— I'm so sorry, mother. I should have listened. I shouldn't have gone out at this hour.

— You did well, my love, said the woman. They bribed you with gifts but you did your task and came home.

Unfortunately, the girl had a younger sister, who had overheard the tale. Gifts? Of course she wanted gifts. She made her way to the mill, in a darkness even deeper than before. And she heard the strain of fiddles, and the racket of laughter. She entered the room where the creatures hopped around the millstone.

— I want you to bring me dresses and jewels and slippers, she told them. And then I promise to dance with you.

They turned those bold red eyes on the girl, and crowded around her. She saw their hairy bodies and cloven feet, and felt a dip in her confidence.

You want us to bring you gifts? Very well.

And they went outside while she waited at the millstone, relieved and dreaming of the riches that would soon come her way.

When the creatures returned, eyes glowing, hooves clipping the stones, in their gnarled hands were not the treasures she expected, but large wooden clubs. And with the clubs they whacked, and thumped, and beat her senseless, their cackling ringing out from the mill to the trees, to the village and to the home where she finally returned, sobbing, ugly and ruined.

The story went around and around in Despo's head as she laid it on the pillow. All was discomfort; her ear hot against the cotton, her hair heavy at the roots. She tried to still her heart. Tried to calm her breathing, against the jagged rhythms of her sleeping husband. She kept her back to him as she wandered, stumbling, anxious, into sleep.

SEVENTH DAY OF
CHRISTMAS

Her dreams had been troubled. She saw herself on a farm she didn't recognise, somewhere in the flatter lands. But it was all empty of animals, and the house was empty, too. From across the fields she could hear a strange mewling sound. She made her way towards it, till she came upon a copper mine. The mewling was coming from inside it. She didn't want to go into that dark place – only men went there – but she had to. Whatever was in there was crying out for help.

She went inside. By the light of the oil lamps, she followed the track until she saw a steel cart, tilted as if it had swerved off course. The mewling was coming from there. And there was scratching. Around the walls, from beneath the earth, a low rumble like a tremor, as if the mine itself was speaking to her, telling her to leave. With caution, she peered into the steel cart. The mewling was coming from a small pink mouth. There was movement, shadow, obscuring the face. It was a goat, a young goat, begging her to save it. She moved her hand to its face and brushed the shadows away, but the shadows had bodies, warm and scaly.

Snakes. She saw now that the cart was filled with them, the young goat crying amongst them. Heart racing, breath tripping over itself, she moved the snakes as they writhed against her skin, as they coiled around her arms and bit her flesh, till she could get a grip on the wounded bleeding animal and lift it out of the cart. She hugged it to her, its small pink mouth screaming, and the snakes coiled around them.

And she woke.

She felt her stomach, convinced of the worst. She lifted the sheepskin off her legs to check for blood and gore, but found only the comforting blankness of a white sheet. A huge breath worked its way up through her body and out of her mouth, the whole length of her, like a spirit being expelled. Her hand went to the other side of the bed, expecting contact with familiar other skin. But Loukas was gone.

The confusion knocked the sleep from her. It still looked dark, but of course it was; winter mornings were austere. So she waited, until the sound of the rooster came.

One.

Two.

Three.

She got out of bed. Her husband was drinking his coffee.

Still unsettled, she went to the stable to check on Manolis. There, the beast stood chomping and nibbling at his hay, over which she signed the cross. She did the same to his sack of feed. And then she held his head, and brought hers to it. That warm, sad face, those big brown eyes gazing into hers. The beast had been in her life for longer than anyone else. She'd played with him when he was just a foal, under his former name, and she recalled how his brown fuzz glowed orange in the June light. He came running when he saw her father, who pretended they spoke a common secret language. The donkey tells great jokes, he'd say, and he'd repeat them to Despo.

I went to the doctor and said, *Doctor, when I touch here it hurts*, and the doctor said, *So don't touch there*. Despo would laugh until her sides hurt. This sweet placid donkey became part of her dowry when her parents died – the only thing they had to give. If anything should happen, at least she had Manolis.

New Year's Eve. The days had slipped away, and yet how long the week had felt. It seemed a lifetime since she'd last smiled.

You never knew where life would go, what the will of God would be from one day to the next. You might plan. You might pray. But all you could really do was start the year hoping for the best. It was the feeling of being lost, the ignorance of what was to come, that was so dreadful. It was the thought that the posts you had pinned your existence to might rot and fall away. The fear that she'd become a mother without her mother to turn to. That she might marry without her father's blessing. That she might be taken out of school to work on the land. The loss of that land. Her separation from her brothers and sisters. Every one of those fears had materialised. She almost cursed herself in retrospect for tempting fate. As if she'd been envious of her own wealth of love and cast the Evil Eye on it.

It did no good to cry. You could only continue living, for your allotted time, with your prescribed amounts of health, peace, joy and love. She still had these things, even if they'd become harder to see.

When the midwife came, they drank coffee and read each other's cups. Domna saw happiness and love in Despo's future. Despo's mind was on other things, so her reading was hazy. She saw nothing. But she said the things everyone wanted to hear, about health and money.

— What's wrong? asked Domna.

— I had a bad dream. It's stayed in my head.

And she retold the dream. Without the horror she'd felt as it unfolded in the night, it sounded little more than a silly story.

— Eh, so you went to bed crazy and had a crazy dream.

— That's what my dad used to say.

— You're worried, my love. The dream was a message from God: don't worry, you're strong. You will protect this new life.

Despo felt something like relief, something like a smile. But she remembered that the fear in her dream was really because she knew she was alone. And alone she'd woken, her husband gone as if he couldn't bear her presence in his bed. Did he really hate her that much? Here she was, doing her best, carrying all the concerns for their child on her shoulders, and Loukas was glad to leave her to it. If this was what marriage was to be, with man as farmer and woman as loaded donkey, then what would come of motherhood? Her back would break in two. She almost wished the pregnancy on Loukas.

— If you have any more of these dreams, let me know, said Domna. We'll take the fear out.

Despo crossed herself.

— Let's hope not.

They talked about the next day. The new year. Discussing the tasks at hand helped to untangle Despo's thoughts. The more she listed chores to be done and ingredients to be got for the table offerings, the clearer with purpose the days ahead became. It pained her to allow herself a small rush of pleasure at the prospect of company.

*

What Loukas liked most about the vineyard was the space to be alone. There on the slope he could survey the island spread out before him. On one side the faraway towns and on the other the villages and orange groves along the coast. There among the vines he was free to sing to himself as he went about his tasks, training his mind on those at the abolition of all other thought, from the burial of grapes in soil to the task that occupied him now: the erection of trellises he had built with his own hands. He'd even chopped down the trees for wood. Over the years, constructing them had become a tonic. The completion of every one a small boost to his value as a real man. He might still be redeemed.

Some of the trellises he'd put up a mere couple of weeks before had been wrecked by the brutal storms. With a heavy heart and a fixed mind, he replaced and secured them all. And from the entrance of the vineyard came an odd noise. A ringing, a bell.

He turned to see Manolis the donkey staring down at the ground unperturbed, and beyond him, at the gate, the Englishman. There he stood, in his brown suit and hat, his silk waistcoat and his crimson bowtie. He kept his bicycle upright with one hand and gave a hesitant wave with the other.

William.

Loukas stood rooted to the soil as the man walked over to him. Crows squawked from the fences.

The man said something in English. Loukas only caught a few of the foreign words, but he understood the meaning from the gaps between them.

The Englishman seemed to change his mind about the conversation. He turned his head.

He commented on the vineyard, looking appreciative.

Yes, it was beautiful. Loukas remembered the word for 'sun', and indicated how the light brought further beauty.

The Englishman removed his hat and passed it from one hand to the other.

Loukas pointed to the scenery beyond the fence. In a mere few months the hills would be starred with anemones, pink and mauve and lilac. And he would have a child to show them to. And Despo would pick bunches for the house, because that had been her first action when they moved in as newlyweds. And the rooms would be filled once again with her singing, when she washed the dishes or rocked the baby in the cot he'd made. It was almost unthinkable.

The Englishman said his name.

Loukas recalled some words in the other tongue.

— *I do not do this.*

The Devil turned his bold blue eyes on him. They were saying that he didn't either.

Needles covered Loukas from head to foot, as if he'd fallen into a patch of prickly pear. He backed away, keeping his eyes on the other man. His wooden cross hung from its thread around his neck. He felt the weight of its protection.

The Englishman continued, his words flying above the peasant's head. But as he talked his body came further down the slope, and then closer to Loukas, until they were whispering, a breath's distance from one another, for the benefit of only the vines and crows. Loukas felt for the knife at his belt.

The Englishman's eyes flicked to it. They looked back at Loukas, and the pain in them, the betrayal, was a stab in itself. Loukas threw his hands at the pale startled face and its eyes glowed, its pupils narrowed, the body at the end of the head juddered as if it was being bled. The Englishman held his heart.

And again, their mouths were pressed together, their moustaches locking, their chests meeting. Again, their hands ventured where they weren't supposed to go. Again, they discarded their clothes and fell, bare-skinned, to the earth. Again, they tasted and touched. Again, they spoke in panicked breaths as if chased by a common enemy. Again, the Devil had won.

*

It had only been a year since she'd played that silly game. She and the other unmarried girls had gathered around the pan by the fire, into which they tossed their olive leaves.

St Vasilis, my king, show me if I'm loved by...

And a name would stay locked in the heart of each, as they giggled and awaited the outcome. One by one the leaves would respond to the coals, and either leap to say yes, she was loved by him too, or curl to convey his dismissal. One of the girls cried when the latter had happened to her. Some of the others teased her. Despo had thought of Loukas. Her olive leaf had leapt.

When her husband came home from the vines, he smelled of earth and sweat. More so than usual. Despo kept her eyes on him as he returned Manolis to his stable and gave him his feed. She signed the cross over the door. He came back into their wind-beaten house, which the constant fire only went so far towards heating, and she served him his dinner, and bowed her head as he thanked God for what He'd so generously provided.

Then he went out again, to the coffee house for a drink and a game of cards.

*

There was comfort in waking the dead. It brought back Despo's mother, placing a coin in the cake for one of them to find. And with her ghost came the children, the ones who'd made it out before the woman's body gave in to the sickness. Before she expelled half-formed half-lives, one tear-stained season after another. Being the eldest, Despo had taken care of all four of her brothers. She had forgone her gifts on New Year's Day so that the boys might have a fraction more to smile about. She had taught them the scraps that had stuck in her head from school before they took her out of it, and she fashioned shoes for them out of rags so that their feet would be better protected from burrs and snakes. She laughed with them as they hopped from cowpat to cowpat in the summer to avoid the scalding earth. And when they buried the second of their parents, she kissed them all goodbye and prayed for their good health. One cousin alone could not provide for five new mouths, so they were split and scattered among the remaining family. The girl, being less required, was sent to a maiden aunt. When she went alone to wash the linen in the river, she would spill the tears she'd saved up in the intervening days. Then she'd beat her anger against the rocks till the wet sheets became a light, damp mass. When she slaughtered her aunt's chickens, she held each one responsible for her fate, plucking each head as if it had decided the course of her life. One day, God willing, Despo would see her brothers again. She wondered if they ever hoped the same.

For now, she had another family: Loukas and his godparents, their children and theirs. The windows were frames of black and the fire spat and crackled. The little ones watched it with a mix of suspicion and awe. In a separate room Agnoulla prepared St Vasilis's table. Between them the women had gathered its components, but she laid them out alone behind closed doors. Olive oil for the Lord's blessing. Wine, Loukas's good batch from a past season, for joy. Fruit and nuts – figs, oranges and loquats, walnuts and chestnuts – for a good crop. Pomegranates for good health. A pouch of gold coins, for the host's pockets to remain full. Agnoulla's own vasilopita, for the family to have bread all year round, containing within it the hidden gold coin that one of them would discover after midnight, and from it be blessed with good fortune. The kollyva, which Despo had made, along with a lit candle, for the peaceful rest of the departed. And finally, the cup and plate from which St Vasilis would eat and drink.

She joined the others again. Eventually, they guessed it to be a quarter of an hour before midnight, and they filled that time with drink and chatter.

— I want a melomakarono, whined Myrto's boy.

— There aren't any, said Myrto, and she slapped his hand. St Vasilis hates sweets. You don't want him to leave without blessing us, do you?

How could the poor boy answer? He could only squirm and make noises like a wounded animal.

— Stop being greedy, his father said, hand and voice both raised.

And when that didn't work:

— You're like a kalikantzaro, wanting nothing but sweets.

The boy whined more, and his mother rolled her eyes. Kleanthis giggled.

— Did you have to? He won't leave us alone now.

— It's all right, my baby, said Agnoulla, who had taken her seat. Come to your grandma, let her bless you with a prayer and they won't touch you.

Kleanthis turned delightedly to Loukas.

— The stories about you are spreading! They've heard them all the way to Damascus by now.

— Leave it, son, said Nestoras. They've all driven him mad with it.

Despo shifted in her seat, but Loukas stared ahead as if his mind and soul had gone for a walk. Kleanthis was enjoying himself too much, and his volume increased with the width of his smile.

— They're saying you fought it, but not just one of them, five! And that you realised what they were because they offered you wine from a golden cup.

— I don't want to see one! cried the boy.

— You won't, my love.

— Don't tell him that, it's not good for him! You might see one. And then you won't be afraid, you'll defeat it.

— Kleanthis, he's still a baby.

— And he needs to become a man. What kind of man is afraid of kalikantzari?

Loukas drank his wine.

— This was a good season, he said of it.

Despo leant over to place her hand on the boy's shoulder.

— Do you know why they come? she asked.

The boy flicked his head: no.

— All through the year, they're underground in hell, and they have saws, and they saw at the tree of life to destroy humanity. But on the twelve days of Christmas they come up here because the waters are unbaptised. And they come to play tricks and torture us. But you mustn't be afraid. You know why?

The boy continued staring at her, but he was still.

— Because while they're up here, the tree of life heals. So when Epiphany comes and the light of God shines on the world, they are the ones who are tortured. They run back down into their hole back to hell. But then they have to start sawing the tree of life all over again. They never manage it, even if they get close. The light always conquers the dark. So you see? They can never defeat us. Never.

After that the boy was quiet, and left his grandmother's lap to play with his sisters.

— My Despina, said Agnoulla, standing, and she kissed the top of Despo's head. God protect you.

The woman went back to the other room, where the saint's table waited.

As the others talked, Despo felt her eyelids droop. She was lulled by the heat of the room, the pleasant sound of human speech, the laughter of the children.

A noise, and a woman's gasp, brought her back to the room.

Footsteps creaked through the floorboards, though no one was walking. The adults whispered to each other. The women were relieved and laughing but quietly so, as everyone watched the children bolt upright at the hearth. Their collective gaze was on the door to the other room, where St Vasilis's table was waiting. From the other side of the door came the muffled voice of Agnoulla.

— Grandma? they asked.

But she was talking to someone and didn't answer.

Then the door swung open. The children cowered.

— That was St Vasilis, she said, stepping into the room. He came and had his fill, blessed our house and now he's gone.

Delighted, the children ran to the room that had so far been locked to them. And there they found a half-drunk glass of wine, the shells of two walnuts and an open window, which they quickly closed and shuttered. Because it was cold, but also to stop anything else from getting in.

EIGHTH DAY OF CHRISTMAS

The past year was over, and may it have taken all the bitterness with it. Outside the church, surrounded by friends and neighbours and all their children, Despo felt the stirrings of hope. Through the bare trees and the wool of the sky, the sun reminded them of its presence. It was only biding its time. Inside the church, in the scent of the incense, in the flicker of candlelight, in the reedy drone of Father Michalis's liturgy, she felt the power of God and the protection of His love. Along with the others, she drank the blood of Christ and ate His body. Just a few more days and the light of God would cast the darkness out.

At the end of the service, Father Michalis called out the names of those who'd had disputes in the previous year. Among them was Christos, followed by Loukas. Despo stared at her husband's back as he made his way to the altar, and at the priest's command held hands with that wild boar. The men put their differences behind them, quickly, and went back to their seats.

— Let's hope he leaves us alone now.

— He'll always want a fight with me. We'll do the same thing next year.

His words settled, and she understood. It brought tears to her eyes to think of her husband defending her honour. The wild boar would keep ramming their door and Loukas would keep chasing it away. So soft a man, and yet so strong. She laughed at his joke and turned to him, to share her thanks, her contentment. But Loukas, unsmiling, kept his eyes on the floor, and when everyone got up from the pews he was the first to leave the church. She struggled to lift herself up.

*

While the children ran off to their godparents to collect their gifts, the women went back with Agnoulla to prepare the meal. The men went together to the coffee shop, where they sat around a table for a game or two of poker. The others had plain coffee, and Loukas had a rose tea. It would be cleansing, he thought.

— Don't tell us you're ill now, said Panikos. Not on New Year's!

— Shut up and play, said Kleanthis.

And as they did, the men slapping their knees, the table, goading each other, laughing, drinking, Loukas saw Pantelis throw his hand up to wave at someone outside. It was the Englishman, dismounting his bicycle. He came in, took off his hat, bade them all a *Happy New Year* in English, and in that same language they said it back to him. Those eyes of his froze on Loukas. But only briefly, for Loukas looked down at his cards and breathed out to cool his face. Then the Englishman was gone.

Good. If Loukas could resist temptation today, it stood him in good stead for the next twelve months. By the grace of God, he would start this year right.

A couple of the men continued to stare at the one departing.

— What's he still doing here?

— What are you talking about? They came to stay, said Nestoras.

— They won't stay, said Kleanthis. We'll get rid of them like we got rid of the Turks.

— They're the ones who got rid of the Turks, you idiot. What are we going to do, pelt them with grapes?

From his usual corner, old Kostakis overheard and tapped his walking stick on the table.

— We thought they were better, he yelled. I remember my father jumping for joy when they came. But now...

— They're all the same.

— A man without shame owns the world.

— That's right.

— *Cheers!* said Panikos in English, laughing, and clinked his coffee cup with Kleanthis's.

— Watch the game, for the love of God! We can all see your cards.

— When the Turks came collecting taxes, the old man continued, if you had nothing, they left you alone. These bastards... they'd try to sell you saucepans on top.

— Things are changing, old man. They'll change again.

— That's right, said Kostakis. Things always change. It's the only thing that stays the same.

The men nodded, as if they'd never heard this before from him. Kostakis was in touching distance of Charon. He could climb a mountain in the morning before the grass was dry, but sometimes he forgot something he'd said only moments ago.

Loukas won the game. They played another, buying a dish of almonds and using them as bargaining chips this time, and he won again. Counting the game of backgammon with Christos the other night, this was his third win in a row. A good sign. A smile from above. The feeling raised his chin to his nose, up to the beams.

After their coffee, the men walked to Nestoras's house. There, another big feast awaited them. It could be like this, thought Loukas, as he took his seat by his pregnant wife and passed the dishes he was passed, and filled his stomach with sausage, bread and wine. Imagine. All year round, to be blessed with food and health and company. There didn't need to be hunger, fear and isolation. It was his fault that things had gone the way they had. Your life was like a crop; it flourished if you put in the work, made good choices, spotted the warnings of failure. Life could be different. Even now, it was not too late. Loukas could be a different, better man. A real one.

*

All around the outside of the house the wind moaned, rattled the windows and poked through the keyholes to be let in. Despo was already asleep in bed – he could hear her gentle snoring. They had sat together in front of the fire for a while, she mending a woollen waistcoat of his, and for a moment he'd felt an unfamiliar sense of peace. She raised her eyes to see him watching. After a fleeting look of surprise, she smiled, and placed her hand on top of his. He chased the lump in his throat with a glug of Commandaria.

From the fire came the pleasing sound of nutshells cracking and twigs chattering as they burned. He tossed in some more shells, a handful of nuts he'd brought home in his pocket from the feast. He remembered to give thanks for the food his godfather's family had provided, which filled his and Despo's stomachs in this darkness of Christmas. God may have awarded little, but it was always just enough.

His gaze lost in the flames, moments from the previous year came back to him: being shaved by the men on the morning of the wedding; being celebrated while a fiddler played on. This was how it felt to be a king, he'd thought, if only for a day. His pride in seeing Despo in her wedding dress, for once demure and speechless. The gleeful anticipation of watching the dough being pummelled and kneaded by her tiny, mighty hands as she made the Easter pastries. The delight in her eyes when she knew she was pregnant, her certainty that she would give him a boy. His satisfaction as he stood back to behold the cot he'd built, with its rocking feet. His plummeting heart at the white stains in the vineyard. The disease. The headless vipers in the woods. Christos coming over to pick a fight in the coffee shop. The rage in his voice, the spit on his chin as he flipped the backgammon board, the way he wanted to throw Loukas to the ground and rip him apart, devour him, obliterate him. But in church, under the priest's benevolent duress, the men had held hands as softly as the boys they once were. The Englishman had held him softly, too. William. William and his hair like fire, the freckles on his shoulders and arms and chest and legs, jumping as his muscles jolted. And William's wife, with her delicate face and the string of pearls around her neck, which she intermittently touched with a small knowing smile. Looking around her. Always taking everything in.

A sensation like myriad holes caving in his heart. He must not think of the Englishman; he ought not to indulge these awful thoughts, these recollections of need and want and – he choked to think it – fulfilment. A sound escaped him. For a moment he thought it had come from outside, but it had come from within. A chilling whine. It brought with it tears and a silent, shuddering misery.

He wiped his eyes on his sleeve.

This would be a good year. Damn him, this would be a good year.

A movement in the flames stopped his thoughts. Not in the flames, above them. It was a thing, not a shadow, but a living thing. He thought of Kleanthis's son, and the leg in the chimney. Was that what he saw? A dark shape, long, cloven at the tip. Disappearing up the chimney, chased off by the flames. Loukas listened closely, through the wails of the wind, and he was certain he heard a soft shuffling, a scuttling, along the chimney breast, up and out onto the roof.

And was that the wind, or was it the strain of violins, deep in the night?

Was it owls in the trees, and cats clawing their way up the trunks, or was it the sound of laughter?

He sat still. He didn't dare blink. He held his breath so that the room made one less noise.

Then he brought his fingers to the cross around his neck, and with the other hand he tossed more nutshells on the fire.

NINTH DAY OF
CHRISTMAS

Despo checked that her torn fingernail was still in the cloth. It crossed her mind to swallow it, just in case, but she decided against it. What she wanted, more than anything, was to get out of the house. But Loukas was out, and the sun, when it finally rose, filled the rooms with a buttery light, and she felt a deep unease. She had spent all morning stitching, and been more productive than she had been through the whole of December, but her work was halted every so often by a distant panic, as if it was coming from a lighthouse somewhere remote, and the thoughts would crowd her mind to break her concentration. She and Loukas had spent a pleasant, if silent, evening in front of the fire; all had seemed better between them. Gone was her tension, the dread of putting a foot wrong, and the resentment that came with it. Gone was the darkness in his eyes. But during the night he'd made noises in his sleep like a wounded animal. They had woken her and kept her awake till dawn. If her husband was infected, he was certain to pass it to her.

Her pelvis screamed. The baby was on its way. She had prayed and prayed for an end, for an answer. She thought of the Virgin travelling thousands of miles to protect her unborn child. But where could Despo go? Even if she did manage to drag herself onto Manolis's back, she would be more at risk outside of the village than here among people she knew and loved. She'd heard more than once of murderers and rapists hiding from the authorities in the mountain forests.

It eased her mind when Aliki arrived. After the service the day before, Domna had said the baby was close, so someone had to be around to help when the time came. Despo's folks were gone and Aliki had no one left. The arrangement suited everyone.

— Maybe we should put her in bed with me, Despo had suggested to Loukas.

— And what if she dies? was his response. She's an old woman.

Despo bit her tongue. Aliki would sleep on blankets by the fire.

On the one hand, the old woman's presence brought a sense of calm. From the minute she arrived, the Armenian fussed over Despo and made sure she was comfortable, and that she had all the food she desired lest the baby was deficient in some way. In preparation she'd made a powder out of crushed myrtle leaves, which she brought in a jar. The thought of patting down her firstborn's pink baby skin rekindled in Despo the joy she'd lately been too concerned to feel. Aliki would also serve as a balm for those silent dinners with Loukas; he would act the engaging host he always did with guests. And though Despo recognised the effort it would take for him to be cheerful, even to speak, she thanked God for some relief from that bottomless sorrow. On the other hand, Aliki's presence was a reminder that the baby was due. And that he might come before Epiphany.

The women sat together to weave baskets. The older one barely had to look at her patterns, so sure was her hand.

— Are you still having nightmares? she asked.

Despo saw in her mind the images from the previous nights. Broken snail shells littering the bed. Dark figures standing with their backs to her, facing the corners of the stable. Her hands cautiously stretching towards them, stretching and stretching and stretching till the fingers were ribbons.

— Yes, she answered.

— What are you eating beforehand?

— Nothing, I stopped eating at night.

— Don't be an idiot, you have to eat. Whatever the baby wants.

— All right, I will.

— We'll take the fear out. I'll fetch Domna and Esme. We'll do it today, so you can have some peace until the baby comes. After the baby comes, don't expect to sleep again!

— Whatever you say. Thank you.

The old woman squeezed her knee and got up to brew them a coffee.

Despo smiled, and hoped Aliki wouldn't die.

*

Loukas did not go to the vineyard, but to the church. He had tossed the thought around in his head all night, and now he was fixed: he would go to confession. He sat in the booth, and it was a long moment before he could speak. There was only his sustained breathing in of the walnut wood, which he fantasised was his coffin, a still-ness he would one day know. He kept his head lowered, and he deepened his voice when at last he spoke.

— Father, I have come to confess my sins.

— Go ahead, my son.

— I have had impure thoughts…

His throat seized. It was nothing he hadn't said before, but this time he felt exposed. Impure thoughts about another man, he ought to say. For it was surely a sin to withhold the truth from a repre-sentative of God, once the truth had been learned. To state it was to give it a form, a body. The name sat on his tongue like a communion wafer. William.

— I have had these thoughts, but I am married.

— I see. My son, thoughts like these aren't uncommon. But they are the work of the Devil, and men are more susceptible to them than women. It's because our needs are greater. For the good of your wife, and your household, you must pray for God's forgiveness.

— They're not about other women.

The words fell out. Not with a clatter, but as a quiet, inevitable descent. Loukas's whole body quivered. For a moment he thought his soul might leave him here as he sat waiting for an answer.

The silence filled his ears, his head.

At last, the priest spoke.

— What did those devils do to you?

Without thinking, Loukas got up and left the confession booth, and his pace picked up as he moved past the eyes of the saints and Jesus bleeding for his sins, until he could no longer hear Father Michalis pleading with him to stop.

*

The shade of the woods made him shiver. But he followed his feet and the sound of water till he reached the creek by the mill. Birds called from branches far above his head. Heaving with air that was too immense for his body, Loukas stumbled over mossy stones and retched by a hedge, his stomach punched by invisible fists, over and over and over, until his chest shook and his teeth knocked against each other, and the tears streamed into his open mouth.

He was sick, and he was contagious. The Englishman was innocent, a victim of the contagion. It was Loukas who'd carried this ill. It was those dead men his father could see in the corners of rooms, the naked soldier on his horse. It was the beings that waited in hedges at the side of the unlit road, to leap out and scare you in the bleak winter nights.

And perhaps it was his child. No, not his child. Surely half-men like him produced fruitless seed. The thing that grew inside Despo wasn't his child at all, but another's spawn. And as it grew its poison spread. It had made her fearful and gloomy, and it had turned him into an abomination. It would be born with stumps for hands, fingers fused like hooves. It would sport a tail and blood-red eyes.

God would not help him now. He had come kneeling, knocking on the door. God had shut him out. He would simply have to live like this. He wouldn't choose death, nor did he deserve it. He refused to commit the ultimate sin. Perhaps the punishment of living alone would be enough for his salvation.

They used to say that in the village, back when there were many more kalikantzari, they strung all the ones they found by the neck from a large cross in the village square, and they cut off all their nails. But as the creatures' nails grew, they were able to free themselves from their confines and escape back into the woods. The villagers learned that if they cut the creatures' nails every so often, they could keep them under control. So that's what they did.

And that was what he would do.

— What's up with you?

He jumped – he couldn't help it. Behind him, stepping through the foliage with his rifle, was Christos.

Loukas flicked his eyes around for a sign of anyone else. For a way out.

— Leave me, Christos.

— There's something going on with you. You're acting like a madman.

— I said: leave me.

— You're talking to yourself. Madman.

Had he been? He had no memory of it.

— And what's this nonsense you've been spreading about us fighting in the woods?

No, no, no. Not here. Not alone among the pines with this man and his gun.

— Are you looking for a fight?

He could hear his own voice shaking.

— Answer me. What's this shit you've been saying?

— I've said it a hundred times. It was Aishe. She wanted…

— Why did you tell her I was here? What were you doing?

— I never mentioned you.

— She says you did.

— And you believed a child?

— I believe her more than you.

Down this road there was only trouble. A rock-slide. A cliff. Loukas softened his tone.

— She misunderstood. She's a child.

Christos raised his rifle, cocked it. Loukas felt the end of his life rush up at him, hell-bent. There was the noise of breath, and boots on the dirt, his hands scrambling for something to hold, and the thud of the gunshot, the sound a thump to his chest. But Christos had aimed away from him. Nearby, a feathered corpse fell through the air and past the pine needles, its landing broken only by sodden twigs.

— Damn you, said Loukas.

Christos spat on the ground, not even bothering to look at him.

— God bless your wife, he said.

*

Despo was not to wear anything red for the exorcism, otherwise the fear wouldn't leave her. Nor was she to wear green, or the fear would return in seven days. She wore black, in the hope that her solemnity would earn God's favour.

Esme and Domna came over after the sun had set, along with a couple of others who only wanted to stick their noses in. Esme carried a cage with two pigeons in it. At first Loukas forgot to hide his annoyance at seeing yet more women in his house, but then, as he had with Aliki, he played the part of the welcoming host. Despo watched his every move.

The women went into the garden, away from the street. They gathered old twigs and dead leaves to build a small fire – thankfully there'd been no rain. There was a saucepan turned over onto the flames and, nearby, a jug of water that had been raised from the well in the dark.

Despo shivered.

Aliki's shawl trembled in the night air. Her right hand came up, unsteady with age, until it rested on top of Despo's head. She began the incantation.

Her fear summoned, Despo dared neither breathe nor blink. It was a dreadful state, to stand firm and conjure in your mind the things that froze your blood in order to face and expel them, but she willed herself to do it. At the edge of the garden she saw something move: a black, scurrying figure, low to the ground. Her heart stopped. Perhaps this was meant to happen. Her fear was being materialised, and she would have to endure it. The terror held her tight, swaddled her body, her throat, her head, her mouth. But the movement came closer, and the birds flapped their wings from the cage, and she saw it was a hedgehog creeping off into the night.

The relief was joyful. She could be such a child at times.

— In the name of the Father, the Son and the Holy Ghost. Amen.

Aliki said the line three times. She then brought over the jug of water and emptied it onto the down-turned pan. It expelled a hiss, like a giant snake rearing up to bite. Despo was to jump over the fire, right foot first. Domna and another of the women held her by each arm to assist, and she went over. She imagined the flames leaping to catch her, or hurt the baby, and the scream jumped out of her mouth. But she had made it over the fire, and the women patted her back. The birds in the cage would absorb her fear, and she would never feel it again.

But then she remembered, and it sliced her breath: she had seen a thing that frightened her, but had forgotten to cross her stomach. She did so now, three times, saying Christ's name and spitting on the ground. She prayed she hadn't touched some part of herself in the meantime, and that God would grant her a child free of ailments.

— What does the pan say? asked Esme. What form did it take?

They assessed the base of the upturned pan, to see how the salt of the water had marked it.

— What is that, a wolf?

— It's a monkey, you idiot.

— No, no, said Domna. I see it, I see it. It's a kalikantzaro.

Despo caught another figure in the corner of her eye. This time it was the man inside the house, watching the group of women from the window. His eyes met Despo's briefly, and then he stepped away from the frame, out of her vision.

— God have mercy, said the midwife, crossing herself.

*

Inside the house, Loukas opened the cupboard where Despo kept her fingernail. He took the folded cloth to the hearth, shook it out, and watched the nail burn.

TENTH DAY OF CHRISTMAS

Together, husband and wife walked to church for the Sunday service. For the first time in his life, Loukas looked up at the cross on its roof with a feeling of dread. Such was the nature of the sickness. It turned a haven into a hell. The symbol of salvation became a sign of refusal.

They took their pews, and he refused to meet anyone's eyes. He let the words of the holy book wash him like a baptism in song. Let him be drowned in God's brutal love. He was safe here on the edges of the room, on the outskirts of the priest's vision. But when the time came for communion, the sweat gathered at his hairline. He ought to be a man and join the line. He ought to eat the body and drink the blood and bow his head to the one who knew his sin. Instead, he felt a flutter in the pit of his stomach. It was an ugly winged thing. It began to flap its way up inside him, and it came to his throat. It was going to push out. It would spill his guts to the floor. He bolted.

Outside the church there was a myrtle tree, at the roots of which he emptied his stomach. This was pain, it was weakness, but it was also a mercy. Purge the bile. Cast the Devil out. It felt like flames at his throat, at odds with the morning dew.

And then a hand was on him, so soft. Despo. His wife rubbed his shoulder and then his back, as if working an ointment into him. She beheld him with all the sorrow of the Virgin.

What had he done to her? What would happen to her now?

She put her arms around him, crouched as he was by the tree, and he allowed her to. Full belly, sprained back, she had lowered herself to cover him, and he held her arms in thanks, in need.

— I'm all right, he said at length. Go back inside.

— I can't leave you like this.

— Go back inside. Take the blessing. The baby needs it.

These were the words she needed to hear. Grudgingly, she loosened her hold on him. He helped her up and, with a hand on her swollen belly, she went back into the church to receive the wafer and the wine.

Above all else came the child. For both of them. It was an innocent, made with God's love – or at least, it would be innocent, and would be loved once it was blessed by Father Michalis. In time it would be baptised and go on to become a good Christian. And if it didn't live long enough for that... Heaven help it. He crossed himself. He would not be a danger to his child, be it boy or girl. He would not allow it to be corroded by him, if the damage hadn't come through his seed already. If there was one thing he could do for his baby, a single act of kindness, a single gesture of fatherly love, it was to leave before it was born.

So he walked. And walked and walked and walked. Past the cemetery, past the dried goods merchants and the coffee house, past the olive groves. His destination was unclear; he would simply follow his feet and allow himself to be guided. Perhaps to the sea, which he saw coolly waving to him in the far distance. Perhaps to the mountains, to live in isolation like the sainted hermit. To battle the demons that made him deaf with their cries. Madman. Christos had been right to call him that.

He hoped he'd got far enough. By the time they left the church, the others would struggle to find him. This was idiotic; he should have gone to the house first, brought the donkey with him. Manolis. He shook his head at his wife's girlishness. She was still so young; she had all her life to live. And she would be all right. The old Armenian was in the house with her now. She would take care of the birth. She'd raised a number of kids of her own, even if it was back in another life, in another place and time. And there was Nestoras to provide for Despo and the child. There was Agnoulla and her daughter-in-law, too, and all the sons to keep them safe.

His throat was dry from the crying. He would stop at a well for water.

*

When she came out of the church, Despo searched the grounds for her husband. He wasn't by the myrtle tree, or at the steps, or on the street. The worry consumed her face.

— Leave him be, said Anthou. If he's sick, you ought to stay away from him anyway.

— Think of the baby, said Agnoulla.

— You have to be calm.

Myrto put her hand on Despo's shoulder. Of course, they were all correct, but there was something in Loukas's reddened eyes that she hadn't seen before. It had thrown a pebble inside her, which rattled around without rest. In the night – she'd either dreamt it or woken to it – his hairy arm had come over her as she slept on her side, and held her. Her arms and her throat. Her stomach. And she'd felt the dark weight at the back of her writhe and spasm, and then go still. The sound that had come out of the man or beast behind her... A pain. A sad, horrible anguish. She'd been wrong to be afraid. He'd been crying for help.

Aliki took her by the arm and the women led her back to the house, reassuring her on the way that her husband was all right. He was a grown man, and in any case, they could take care of him if need be.

She had only to think of the baby, which would be coming now, any minute.

As they left the hallowed grounds she cast her eyes back again. For a sign, for some comfort. Father Michalis was watching her, and he signed the cross in the air to bless her from afar.

Back at the house, Aliki forced her to sit down and do nothing while she brewed some chamomile.

— Don't worry about him, she said to the girl.

After all, those wrinkled brows were for no one else's sake.

— I know, said Despo, I shouldn't. But...

She didn't know what she could say, or how much. But even if she was free to open her mouth and spill out every word she knew, how could she possibly arrange them to form her feelings? She barely understood what she felt, or why she was afraid.

— It's been a while, she said at last. He's been ill for a while. And I've only just realised.

— What do you mean?

The old woman poured the tea.

— Sometimes... It's as if his spirit leaves. He sits there, chewing like a goat, staring at nothing. There's no... light. His spirit goes.

Aliki nodded.

— We can't always be dancing, she said. Loukas is the type who gets lost in his thoughts. You can

143

see it in his eyes. His brain is humming, and he can't hear much else over it.

To her own surprise, Despo's tears ran.

— I just want him to be well. Sometimes he is, and you can feel the difference. When I see him smile, I know he can be happy. He can. But I can't keep that happiness going. There's something I'm not doing. Me. It's my fault.

— Listen to me: a dog's tail never straightens. There's nothing he can do even for himself – it's who he is. So what could you possibly do, you poor thing?

— Be a good wife.

— And you think you aren't? You love him, you take care of him, you cook his meals, clean his house, do your work to bring more money, and now you're having his baby.

— And it's not enough.

The old woman squeezed her knee.

— I'm telling you, it's enough. Drink your tea.

The girl lifted the cup to her mouth, but neither her lips nor her eyes moved so much as a millimetre.

— Get this into your head: light will come and go. When the darkness comes, you make a fire, put on clothes... You protect yourself. You know you'll be cold, you know you won't see well. But then it goes away. The only thing you have to do is remember that it comes back. You get ready for it and face it again. But you know it always goes away again, too. Because the light always comes back, as well.

The old woman's words lingered for a while, some of them settling and some of them floating away. Nothing could combat the feeling in Despo's gut, the certain knowledge that something was terribly wrong.

Before the sun set, she placed a colander on the doorstep. It would distract the creatures, who would grow obsessed with counting the holes.

By the time Aliki had prepared their dinner, there had still been no word from Loukas. People had dropped in throughout the afternoon, and into the evening, to check on her and ask after him. What could they say? Some came with information: he wasn't at the coffee house; he wasn't at the vineyard or the orchards. He was seen by Mehmet heading beyond the well. Christos had come round. He'd been to the mukhtar's house, and asked him to speak to the Englishman on their behalf.

— The Englishman? What's he going to tell us? Aliki had asked. He doesn't even know the cats here.

— They're friends, Christos spat back. Her husband and him.

— Friends with the foreigner? You're talking nonsense. They can barely speak two words to each other.

— Loukas looks after his orchards, said Despo in a small voice.

— That doesn't mean they sit down with a teapot, love.

Christos was about to add something, when Despo interrupted.

— So? Did the mukhtar speak to him?

— He's not home. The Englishman. He's not there.

Christos had said this with meaning.

— Let her rest now, said Aliki. This isn't good for the baby.

— It's you, said Despo.

The man turned his wolfish eyes on her.

— What?

— You've done something to him.

— What are you blabbering about?

— You hate him, you were fighting him!

His eyes glinted, but his hairy hand came to his heart.

— I swear to God, I never fought him. Shut your mouth.

She wouldn't, not now. It felt too good to let her anger out, to raise her voice back.

— You put the Eye on us, I've known it for ages. Get out of my house! Get out before I kill you.

— You're crazy, said the man. Ask the Englishman what he knows. Crazy woman.

— Get out!

— Crazy man married a crazy woman.

— Enough, said Aliki. Go.

And she saw Christos out of the house, reluctant as he was to leave and large as his body was to push through the door.

— Don't listen to him, she said. What could that foreigner know?

*

The sun was dipping behind the mountains, and the village was far behind him. Again, Loukas cursed himself for not taking the donkey. If only the Swedes were still around with their vehicles, to ferry him elsewhere quicker. Perhaps to the towns. If only he'd thought to take William's bicycle. Not that he knew how to ride it. With the setting of the sun, he felt a lifting of his spirits. Alone in a field, with no other being as far as the eye could see, he was free to be what he was. A harmless devil. A fallen angel. A man whose desires affected no one.

There were other men like him. He'd heard jokes about them all his life. He'd even heard tales of gods and poets who felt his kind of love – Greeks who travelled to Alexandria to spend their afternoons behind shutters with brown-skinned boys. In the frankness of the open air, without buildings and costume and craft, he was able to face the truth of himself. And it told him who he was: a man who had never felt more for a woman than friendship; a man who had dreaded consummating the marriage as much as his young bride had; a man who felt for other men what he was supposed to feel for women. He had been born with a defect, and it wouldn't change. He would go to hell and it didn't matter. Nor did it matter if he lived alone, wandering from village to village, through olive groves and vineyards, along the coast, for the rest of his life. Life was appetite. Nothingness was death.

He didn't want to die.

On either side of him were fields of wheat, swaying in the hush of twilight. And then the sky went black, and the road went grey. The only sounds were his footsteps on the dirt and the nightjars croaking nearby. He hadn't a torch, not so much as a matchstick. And then another sound came: his growling stomach. He realised he hadn't eaten since noon, when he'd come upon a blackberry bush and picked to his heart's content. How foolish it had been not to bring more with him. Part of him had hoped to find a sanctuary by now; had hoped that some miracle might guide him.

Ahead, there was movement. He broke his walk and stood still, waiting. And from the corner of his eye he saw a spread of feathers, and heard the swoop of an owl catching a rodent in its talons. He swore under his breath, hand at his heart. He crossed himself.

This was as far as he should travel for one day. He ought to find a safe spot to sleep, cold though it was beneath the stars. So he lay against an olive tree, fat with age, and put his head against a rock. This was his punishment, not to be in bed with his wife, in a house where the fire had been going since Christmas Day. Then—

Could it be...?

He raised himself from the ground, dusted off his vraka. Silence, but something else as well. He walked a few paces.

From beyond the tall silhouettes of cypress trees came the faint sound of music. Laughter. The cold air seeped into his bones. His heart dropped to his feet, and his feet gripped the ground. His breath stopped so his ears could listen. His lashes stilled so his eyes could see. But all he could make out were deepening shades of blue and black. With caution, he moved towards the trees. The strains of the fiddles grew louder, and so did the merriment.

Eventually, he reached the source of it. There behind the trees was a creek; he crossed its little stone bridge to a field and a threshing floor on the outskirts of a village he had never seen before. There were fiddlers, and people dancing in the light of oil lamps. There was a bride and a groom: she in a white lace dress and he looking proudly out at the party. Most pleasing to his eyes, there was a long table laden with food. His stomach moaned at the sight of it. One of the dancers turned and noticed him hiding behind the cypress. The man beckoned to him.

Loukas could no longer ignore his hunger. He made his way to the gregarious man, who had a large black beard and a brilliant red waistcoat. The man hobbled on the uneven ground to meet him halfway.

Eat, he said to Loukas. Fill yourself up – you're skin and bone.

Loukas did so. Spread out on the table was an array of carcasses. Pheasant and chicken and lamb. The scent of a hog on a spit was like skewers at his nostrils. He gorged on the food, picking at it and stuffing it into his mouth. There was also wine, which the hosts poured into cups and passed around. In the flickering light, the cups looked an odd shape and the liquid an unknown hue. But he drank, and it was exactly as wine should be. With a hint of earth, and a tangy taste, something beyond the notes of grape.

Welcome, said the groom, who'd walked over to him, too. His moustache was thick, and stiff with wax.

Was he having a good time?

Of course. This was the miracle Loukas had prayed for.

The groom put his hand on Loukas's shoulder. His palm, like the hairs at his lip, was damp with sweat.

Dance with us.

Together they leapt into the middle of the threshing floor, where men moved their arms through the air like windmills, where they draped those arms around each other's shoulders and kicked the dust off the ground as if to banish yesterday. Winter was outside this circle. Within this light was brotherhood.

The bride's lace dress moved to the edge of his vision. Loukas followed its train to the creek. There on the bank, the dress lifted up at the front, and a glittering stream arced into the water.

Stunned, Loukas turned back to face the groom.

The man was smiling at him. And his hand moved from gripping his shoulder to stroking his nape, gently, firmly, pulling him closer.

ELEVENTH DAY
OF CHRISTMAS

The last of her mother's pregnancies had been more hopeful. Like its predecessors, the baby had made it to the final term. But while the others had failed to do so, this one would live beyond its first few days. Despo was sure of it. On the morning her mother's waters broke, her grandmother sent her to fetch the midwife. The bedroom filled with women, each of them praying for a smooth labour. But as her mother pushed and pushed, knuckles white from her grip on the birthing seat, it became apparent that something was wrong. The midwife summoned Despo's father. The girl had never seen him in the room during a birth. He came to do his duty. He said the Lord's prayer three times, knelt to sign the cross three times, and left. At the midwife's instruction Despo and the other women unbolted the doors, and opened cupboards and wardrobes and drawers so as to encourage her mother to open. Some time passed before this worked. A black-haired head appeared between her mother's legs. But the midwife's expression turned, and Despo knew at once the child was dead. After a panicked few minutes, the worst fear was confirmed. The cord had wrapped around the baby's neck in the womb. She hadn't even taken her first breath.

The memory circled Despo's mind. If her birth was a difficult one – God forbid – would Loukas even be there to do his duty? She had spent all night awake at the fire to keep it going, with an ear ready for his footsteps and a bowl of soup awaiting his spoon. She didn't even know if he'd return at all. If he did, would she run to him with open arms? Or would she twist the head off his neck?

*

Loukas woke up beneath the olive tree. His neck was sore from the rock he'd leant against; his arms were scratched from rubbing against the bark. But he was thankful, for at least he hadn't frozen to death in the night. What an end to his life that would have been, to be discovered by a worker in the fields, far away from anyone who would have known him. They'd have buried him there and then, or left his corpse to the birds.

Images resurfaced inside him. Those people. The wedding party. His head was pounding.

As his mind pulled away from sleep, he became aware of a stench. There was his own unwashed, exhausted body, but there was also another, more pungent, smell. He looked behind him. The rock he had been resting his head against was not the usual shape, not the usual texture. Neither were the ones near it. And then he realised they weren't rocks at all. They were hooves.

He leapt up. The breath erupted in him as he saw, splayed out on the ground with its entrails pecked and a tangle of maggots wriggling inside it, the rotting carcass of a donkey.

*

The Englishman had no idea where Loukas had got to, and there was no reason to disbelieve him. He'd looked truly saddened. Some of the men went out on horses to search the outskirts, the fields, the woods, even the nearest villages. From Christian Greek to Moslem Turk, Maronite to Roma, across the peaks and valleys not a single soul could help.

Despo's breath flapped like wings. Aliki made tea and tucked her into bed with woollen blankets. She must think of the baby's health, and not give in to panic. It was all the old woman could do: hold the girl and sing to the baby kicking in her stomach. It brought a melancholy joy to her face to remember those rhymes of the East which she had sung to her own children, all those years ago. Neighbours dropped in to see them. Agnoulla, Myrto and Kiki brought dishes of food so that neither Despo nor Aliki depleted herself. They sat around the bed dunking rusks in tea, mostly in silence. And occasionally the abandoned woman would cry to the walls.

— Where has he gone? What's happened to him?

What could the others say? No answer would bring her comfort.

In the afternoon, when the others had left, Aliki set to baking, and it struck her as a fine idea to get the girl to help. As expected, the activity went some way towards calming Despo. Her hands moved by memory to make the mixture, knead the dough and divide it up. Method pleased the mind, and hands were grateful for work.

The church bells chimed. Aliki looked up and crossed herself. She watched the window as if something was there, but it was only trees and sky. Then, in a click of the fingers, Despo understood. The bells were solemn. Languid. Someone was dead.

The images gathered in her head at such a pace it made her dizzy. Her vision went white. Someone would come to announce that her husband's body was found, that Loukas had been face down in the creek. At last the tears streamed down her cheeks, and Aliki held her hand.

— It's him, the young woman said. It's him.

Her lungs were full of thorns, her throat full of holes. Aliki held her by the shoulders and shushed her like a baby.

— We don't know yet, she said.

Soon, they did know. Myrto had come running to give them the news. She held the pregnant woman's hands, as much to steady herself as the one she was giving the news to. Her eyes were wide with sadness and fear.

— It's Domna.

At first, Despo failed to understand.

Aliki gasped and put her hand to her mouth. She and Myrto watched the mother-to-be as the words went in.

The midwife was dead.

Despo's legs spasmed, but the women held her upright. After a moment's confusion, she felt a sudden clarity. Her eyes were drying. She went straight to the cupboard and took out the small cloth. She unfolded it, with a careful but shaky hand. The fingernail was gone.

*

For as long as there was an open grave, the pregnant woman was not to sleep. But how would Despo even shut her eyes, with the midwife gone and her husband vanished? Night had fallen and Loukas had yet to return. Aliki had made chickpeas for them to eat and his seat remained empty. Domna was wrapped in a winding sheet and Despo may as well have worn a widow's veil.

They said the midwife's heart had given out, God rest her soul. One minute she was fine, the next she'd dropped to the floor, spilling the kollyva she'd made for her father's memorial. She'd be buried in the morning.

When the sorrow cleared, Despo was left with a strength she thought she'd lost. It held her up like a pillar. In that moment, she saw it, plain as the bread on the table: her husband had left her. She had always been the reason for his sorrow, and he had chosen now to save himself. It had happened to other women, with or without child. Why not her? What had led her to believe she was blessed? She held her stomach and rocked herself. It was already written. The shape of her family was always to be God, the baby and her. Loukas was only ever to stand outside of that union.

He was the one to put himself there. Not her, not the baby, not God. Bitterness sat on her tongue, a nuisance tea leaf. All these months of pain and worry, only to be dealt another portion by the absence of a man who'd been absent throughout. Never had he given himself to her, not the way she had to him. Rarely had her husband returned the comfort he sapped. Was she crying for him, for fear of his welfare, or was she crying for herself, the idiot, for the loss of something she'd never had? A mist came over her eyes – not mist, smoke, with its stinging ash.

She snapped her eyes open. It had only been a second. She assured herself she had only blinked.

Aliki snored beside her on the hearth. Despo watched the fire. Every so often she would stoke it, if only to keep herself occupied. She did so now and her heart leapt; the shadow of a flame jumped, like a leg hopping back up the chimney.

And then an image came to her: her husband's face, looking on in fear. Where had she seen that? When was it? Eventually she recalled it. She went to the bedroom and even in the dark her hands found their way to the baby's waiting cot, and the clothes lying there in wait for him. Among them, the woollen socks the Englishwoman had made. Despo took them to the fire. She would throw them in and break whatever curse they'd put on her husband. But she hesitated. She looked at the small fabric feet in her palm, which would soon wrap around her baby's limbs. She felt the warmth of another woman's arms embrace her. Holding the socks to her chest, she returned them gently to the wooden cot and wiped her eyes clear.

There was something else she could do. Pelvis burning, she stood at the table to make xerotiyana. A night too soon, but such was the state of things. Having prepared the pastry, she filled a pan with olive oil over the fire and hoped it wouldn't wake Aliki as she threw spoonfuls of the mixture into it. They crackled pleasingly; the smell hugged her heart. But perhaps she should have been more cautious and not made them at night, not so close to the chimney, in any case. She spooned the fried pastries out onto a dish and poured honey over them. Then she went into the pantry for the sausage and cut it up into pieces. Tonight. She would do it tonight.

Taking a deep breath, and carefully so as not to wake Aliki, she opened the door and stepped outside. She saw only the stars, heard only the owls. In the snapping cold she clutched her cross. She surveyed the neighbourhood. There were only the silent houses, each with its own fire burning through Christmas.

She stepped back to view her house. Nothing on the roof. One by one, she threw the pastries onto it, along with the morsels of sausage. Most of them had struck their target, ending up close to the chimney. The relief brought tears to her eyes as she said the requisite words.

> *A little piece of sausage,*
> *A black-handled blade,*
> *A little piece of pastry,*
> *Now eat and go away.*

TWELFTH DAY
OF CHRISTMAS

From his vantage point, the Englishman saw a clear path. Below was all the land, spread before him, as if for him. He made out groves and fields, a makeshift camp, the coastline. Thus far, the villagers' searches for the missing winemaker had brought up nothing. So he'd bidden farewell to his wife with some excuse, got on his bicycle and gone on his own hunt. No sooner had he set off than he felt a pain in his chest, and for a moment he panicked. His old failing: the man had been born with a hole in his heart. It had kept him from fighting in the war. There were nights in those long-ago school dorms when he'd wake in a panic, sweat cooling on his legs, and he would hold his chest as imagined blood gushed from the hole. The other boys knew of his ailment, and so they thought less of him. He was excluded from games. Nobody asked him about his ability, or the boundaries of his comfort. They decided he was limited, and that's how they treated him. He didn't dare tell them of his other condition.

Loukas, that gentle other being with those depthless black eyes, was the only one who'd ever known of it. If nothing else, they had it in common. He was real, he had to be, and by God he would be found. Where could anyone start? Loukas had left no clues. He hadn't even taken his donkey, which suggested his sudden departure was due to impulsiveness or abduction. William had heard tales of bandits hiding in the mountains. It was likely the man whose body had once been warm against his now lay cold in the woods.

On the one hand, the thought tortured him. On the other, it brought relief.

How could he achieve what other men had failed to achieve? They knew the land better than he did, they spoke its dialects. They also knew Loukas. The Englishman knew nothing of him apart from his lips, his hands. He willed himself to be led by something – if not God, then some thread, leading through the labyrinth – but in the rising daylight there was only the grass being stroked by the winter air.

Out of nowhere, he felt a stinging in his eyes. What had he come here for? He had no idea what he was doing. All he'd gained was more trouble. He cleared his throat, his eyes.

The coast. He would head for the coast.

As he took the downward slope towards the fields, he felt a soaring within. He might crash his cycle and die, his life ceased by a rock, and perhaps that would be best. It was the opposite of misery he felt in these fleeting visions; it was release. Just as when he lowered his face to that creek in the woods, on that fateful day Loukas came running towards him.

The road had straightened, but it was not smooth. The sound of his bicycle was the only noise along the path, until he neared the camp he'd spotted from the hill. Then he heard the voices of smoking men, and the crying baby in the arms of a woman who turned to face him with large gold eyes, large gold hoops through her ears. A stabbing ache. The foreigner shivered, his hand going straight to his heart. There was no blood at his chest, no leak. There was only a murmur, a voice, a breath through its perforation. The dark figures with their tents and horses watched him as he passed, but that was all.

How stupid he had been. To think he could come here and know the place. To think that Loukas, the Cyprian, was the one in danger, when this was at least his home.

*

The funeral procession was to pass outside the house. Aliki made sure that Despo was nowhere near it. She was to stand in the other room, and not lie down until the deceased was buried. Despo stared out at the garden. The pomegranate tree, the loquat. The cherry. Soon the blossoms would come, and the anemones would cover the mountainside.

They would bury the logs from the fire to protect the house, the yard, the stable, the vineyard. She would sit outside in the spring breeze, nursing her little boy. This darkness would go. It always did.

She saw the outhouse, which she'd avoided using after sundown ever since that night she'd heard the scratching. How insignificant it looked now, in the blank light. And she saw the stables. Manolis chomped his feed.

— I won't go, said Aliki. You need me here.

— No, go. For me, please go.

— I can't leave you.

— I'm fine. The baby's resting. He won't come now.

It was only for the funeral. And only one more day till this was all behind them for another year.

Aliki was reluctant, but she nodded, and covered her hair with a shawl.

— Don't lose your head when your waters break, you hear me? The baby will come long after that.

She left, and Despo was truly alone. She waited till the cries of the mourners evanesced before she went to the front room to sit and stoke the fire. She threw more nutshells on the flames to keep them satisfied. The house was empty; the only sounds were the cracks and spits. It was only for today, and only for now. Aliki would be back in a matter of hours. Women would gather in the bedroom in no time. The baby would fill the house to the ceiling beams with his cries before she knew it. Isolation had never bothered her before. Why was it so unwelcome now?

She took control of herself, and went outside to breathe some air. Although it was daytime, she approached the stables with caution. She could hear Manolis's low sighs, the rustle of his hooves on the hay. At least Loukas had left her the donkey. His sober face made her heart melt. She held it to hers, embraced it as she wept. It wasn't the cold that made her shake. Here with the donkey she was warm, warmer than she'd felt in a long, long time.

Loukas had left her the donkey. Something in her mind clicked into place like a lock.

Her husband was dead.

If he'd meant to leave, he would've taken it. No one had reported any missing animals. The Englishman only had a bicycle. The Swedes had been gone for a month, and taken those strange black vehicles with them.

Her fingernail had been stolen.

Her midwife had died of a failed heart.

Her husband had come to harm.

Despo heard it before she looked down and saw, from the darkening hay on the floor, that her waters had broken.

Don't lose your head, Aliki said in her ear.

For a moment she stood still. Her fingers quivered against Manolis's pelt. Then she latched onto him – he

169

must let her, she had to climb onto his back somehow and find someone to help. The ache in her back, her pelvis, it was too much. Her teeth ground against each other, blocking her sobs. The donkey brayed as she clutched him, but it was no use; she couldn't lift her veiny legs to mount the beast, she could not lift herself and her weighted stomach beyond a desperate rise to the tips of her toes. The donkey couldn't carry her from danger. Not while she was alone.

Hugging her stomach, she staggered back to the house, recalling Aliki's words. Don't panic. Don't panic. The baby would come later. He would wait until the rooster crowed three times on the morning of Epiphany. She would stay in the house and brew herself a chamomile tea for the crippling pains in every part of her, until someone, anyone, came to her aid.

When she went back inside, there was a figure in the front room. A gasp escaped her. There before her eyes, as real as anything else in the room, was a woman she'd never seen before. Old, her face pock-marked by some past illness. Her clothes were so worn that the threads barely held together.

The door was open, she said. She'd let herself in. She didn't mean to scare the girl.

— Who are you?

The woman looked down at the swollen stomach and clapped her hands together with glee. She asked how far along Despo was, and Despo told her.

— Who are you? Despo repeated.

The woman said she'd come from the next village. She'd heard the girl was in need of a midwife. What had happened?

So Despo told her of Domna's death. The woman nodded sagely and seemed sad, though her damaged face kept half of her mouth pulled up in a strange mocking grin.

— Would you like something to drink? Despo asked, and she set to brewing a chamomile tea.

She guessed from the bony wrists and unwashed clothes that the old woman was hungry, and certainly poor. So she sliced up the loaf of bread and spread it with butter and honey. As expected, the old woman champed at it with zeal, licking the honey off her long, thin fingers. And she asked where Despo's husband was.

Despo said she didn't know, and the woman held her hand. It was still cold from outside.

She didn't want to talk about Loukas as if he was dead, or bear the shame of a stranger's pity, so she spoke of him as if he was on the point of coming home. He was at the funeral now. Normally he would be at the vineyard, or making vinegar, or racking wines in the cellar. The woman was intrigued. She was very fond of wine – her late husband had also grown grapes. She asked if she might see the cellar. Despo had a better idea: she would gift her a bottle for assisting with the birth.

— It's good of you to come.

It was no problem.

— How did you find out?

They told me.

— Who?

I don't know them, love. I'd never met them before.

The old midwife helped her up. A sharp pain in Despo's spine made her wince.

It was better to move, she said, not to sit still for too long.

Despo knew she ought to rest, but she certainly couldn't lie down as long as there was an open grave in the vicinity. So she listened to the ragged old woman, who suggested they go to the cellar. Despo led the way.

Then she stopped, because the house felt cold. Shivering, she looked over to the fire, which had fizzled to embers. Her heart almost burst. She went to stoke the fire. When that did little, she held some kindling to a lamp that was still lit, thank God, and held it to the embers. There was still the night to get through – this had to work. But the flames would not take. The thorny log was damp to the touch.

Despo controlled her breaths.

Leave that, said the stranger. Let's go to the cellar and then we can start the fire.

— Go down yourself, said Despo. I'll take care of this.

The woman didn't know where it was. Despo would have to show her.

Why was the log damp? What was that smell?

Let's go. Come on.

The pregnant woman knew she ought to do as she was told.

Together they descended to the cellar, the midwife taking the oil lamp. The cold struck Despo even more as she walked down the stairs. She crossed her stomach and then held herself, covering her chest and shoulders as best she could. While she did so, she felt her shawl for a piece of string. They went slowly, Despo placing a careful foot, one after the other, on each step down. The place was dark despite the warm pool of light. And there was that rich aroma of the wine. Loukas would once have stood here, and she prayed he would do so again. The smell of wine began to sour. More and more so, until the smell came closer to urine. Was that why the log was damp? In the cramped space, she knew that the smell wasn't coming from the wine, but from the old stranger behind her. Pregnancy made the stench more intense. She recalled the earlier months, when neighbours brought bites of the dinners they cooked, lest the smell from afar should harm the baby.

She took a bottle of wine from the racking and handed it to the old woman – God willing it would get her out of the house. Together they went back up, but the midwife insisted Despo lead the way again. This way, if she should have a fall, the woman would break it. Despo expelled breaths through her nose and tried not to breathe in, as step by step she made her way back up. Behind her, the stranger's feet clomped up the steps. Despo would go ahead. She would pick up her pace, and when she reached the top she would turn and slam the door. The light above came closer, and her heart hurt, closer still, and her back hurt, and her teeth clacked together in the chill, and then came a pain in her stomach, so strong it brought her down to her knees. The step grazed her shin.

The baby's coming, said the midwife.

— No, whispered Despo. No, no, no...

She pulled herself up the rest of the way, one knee after the other up the steps. And when she reached the top, the midwife overtook her, and she dragged her with those bony fingers by the arms across the floor to the hearth, where the fire was finally dead. The piece of string had left her palm – where had it gone? Where was it? Despo smelled urine again, but this time it wasn't coming from the other woman. She howled in agony.

— Help me up, she said. I can't lie down. I mustn't lie down.

So the midwife yanked her up, and a flame shot through Despo's spine. The words shuffled out with her ragged breaths.

— Where's your birthing chair?

The midwife hadn't brought one.

— Go fetch one. Go get someone. For the love of God.

She didn't need a birthing chair. Despo could kneel, and the baby could rush out that way, too.

— He won't come now.

Her shredded breaths.

Of course he'll come.

— No.

He's on his way.

— No. Tomorrow. Please God, tomorrow.

But she knew before the midwife responded that it wouldn't be tomorrow.

No. Now, said the old woman.

Despo looked to the door, where the wooden cross hung, and she prayed for someone to step through it. Aliki. Loukas. Domna's wandering spirit. Next to the cross was the black-handled knife. If only she could reach it.

The old woman made her kneel, and forced a hand between her legs. She asked for cloth and scissors, but Despo only answered with a sob. The midwife went to fetch them herself. Despo tried to get up. She would get on her feet and grab the knife. But she couldn't; her legs collapsed. The old woman came back with a bowl of water, Despo's scissors and a cloth. She brought another rag and told her to bite down: the baby was coming. Those cold bony fingers between her legs again, and Despo screamed. She hadn't crossed her stomach, or spat on the ground, or said the Lord's name. She'd touched her body, despite her fright. And now it was too late – the boy was coming.

— You can't have my baby, she whispered, the tears streaming down her face.

Hush now.

— Please.

Hush.

Loukas's rifle leant against the wall. Her lost, wandering husband. He wasn't even armed against Them.

He's coming, the midwife said, and Despo felt it.

Her baby's head was emerging. She screamed into the damp rag, and gradually, painfully, her body split open, his little body slid out and out, into the air, and into the midwife's waiting hands.

A boy. A boy. A boy.

The midwife snipped the cord and bound the stump at the baby's navel. From the fireplace she brought a poker, bold red at the tip, and held it to the wound.

The baby cried.

— Give him to me, said Despo. Please, let me have my son.

Had the midwife even wiped his mouth? His cries were gargled; he was choking on the mess.

Despo's energy seeped out of her like blood. Her body begged for rest, her eyes for sleep. The knife was far from her reach. But on the floor by her knees was the pair of scissors. And, gripping her cross in one hand, she picked them up with the other. The old woman held the baby to her bosom, brought him to her pockmarked face, to the mouth that warped into a grin, and Despo brought the scissors through the air, straight to the other's throat.

The midwife juddered. Turning to the light, she looked already long dead. Skin and bone, freshly exhumed. She sputtered, dribbled, and went still. Then, noiseless as bedding, the dead woman fell against the living one, who snatched the child from the lifeless arms and held him tightly to her heart.

Her boy.

Her boy.

Her boy.

*

They found her not long afterwards. Aliki returned from the wake with Agnoulla and the others, thank God. At first, they saw the blood across the hearth, and among it a pile of rags encasing a body more skeleton than woman. The blood even draped a creature slumped against a chair, its clean exposed breast nursing a baby. Aliki ran to the new mother, who looked up, eyes wide and wet with thanks, dripping with another's blood, before her lids gave up, and shut. And for the first time in days, Despo drifted into sleep.

EPIPHANY

Her son was alive, glory be to God. She named him Fotis.

When she'd woken up in fresh sheets, bathed and smelling of lavender, for a moment Despo sensed that all had been a dream. The winter sun was hazy in the window. The dew eventually cleared from her vision, and she saw Aliki sitting by her bed with a bundle in her arms. She heard the sounds of her baby, and saw his face, clear and beautiful, the face of an angel, as Aliki brought him to her. She held him. Inhaled him. Kissed him. Spilled her tears on his cheeks and wiped them away. Her son.

Dalaili-dalaili
The bird sat down
Upon the branch

The lullaby she'd once sung to her brothers.

And he wanted a kiss

She gave her child a kiss. And many more as the song went on. Her boy.

They had rubbed him with salt for strong bones. They had washed it off with blessed water. They had bandaged his limbs so they would grow straight and well. They had wiped his lashes with candle ash for black brows. He had no deformities, no marks on his skin. He was alive, and long may he live.

Men had disposed of the old stranger's corpse. They decided it had been a beggar from another village, looking for babies to steal.

*

Only God knew how long Loukas had walked for. And only God knew where he was.

The sound of the sea rushed towards him. He half-walked, half-stumbled down the dunes, and he pulled off his boots to feel the beachgrass brush his feet. Despite the sun the sand was cool and wet, and the breeze spat it back at his skin. It was only when he reached the shore and offered his toes to the waves fanning out to grasp the land like a hungry ghost that he knew what day it was. And he knew it because of the gathering taking place not two hundred yards from him. At the centre of a crowd of half-dressed men was a priest. Even from this distance, Loukas picked out words from the passages he'd heard throughout his life. God created the world. He made the waters. Eve succumbed to temptation and Jesus was baptised in the River Jordan. There couldn't have been a clearer sign.

He walked, then trotted, then ran towards the ceremony. He had angered God, and God had tested him in return. He had placed that English devil before him and Loukas had bitten the apple. Lusted in his heart and spent his seed. And God had been just in his sentence. Loukas had bled, and cried, and felt the crippling hunger of a life outside the light. Here was redemption.

The priest sang his psalm and blessed the waters. The sea rolled grey and blue, retreating and returning, waiting, like a dog expecting a bone. And then the cross left the holy man's hand. It spun gracefully into the sky and landed with a splash in the sea. The men set off.

Heart pounding, Loukas sprinted into the water. Numb from his nights in the fields, he barely felt the punch of the freezing waves. The other men thrashed about him in the sea. He felt their tugging at his legs, his chest, his arms as he swam closer, salt in his throat, closer, his worn-out limbs on fire in the water, closer to the cross sinking deeper into the blue. A finger at his eye, a fist at his temple. And in his head was Despo, in his heart their child. He knew with a sudden clarity that no matter what he would make his way back to them. Despo had only ever loved him, and would only ever love him. He could love her, too. Maybe not an all-consuming love, but one that comforted and warmed like the waistcoats she made and mended for him. At the very least he could be kind to her. If the child was a boy, Loukas need not be afraid. Men were not all the same. Whether boy or girl, a child deserved love. And he had it within him; he was not a well of hate, not merely a place of darkness. There was light in him, too. If Loukas was blessed by winning the cross, then may God bless them all. He pushed and pushed through the water, until… His fingertips touched the wood. His hand curled around it. Something struck his shoulder and made it slip from his grasp. Feet at his chest, at his arms, at his chin. But he caught it. It was his.

He soared to the surface, which he pierced with the cross in his outstretched hand. The sea air whistled around his head, and he wept tears of joy. He had won. The other men resurfaced, slapping the sea in frustration. And every single one of them, slick and exhausted, regarded Loukas in awe. Who was this man? How did he get here?

And on land, from among the dunes, rose a figure. He grew from the ground. That brown suit. That waistcoat. With that unmistakable hair atop the slim, pale body, the Englishman looked like a votive candle planted in the sand. Here was his prayer, answered.

The surge of joy in Loukas's heart flushed tears from his eyes. They mingled with the saltwater. The other men continued to stare at him, and he loved them. He was filled with love, for perhaps the very first time in his life. He brought the cross to his face and kissed it, laughing, shivering. He had won. He closed his eyes as he raised his head to the sun, to feel the warmth of God's light upon him.

Acknowledgements

The Vassiliou family: Panayiotis for his immense knowledge of Cypriot life, history, proverbs, songs and traditions (his book *Δαυλός* was an invaluable resource); Christalla for her food, hosting skills and anecdotes of life in the village; Natasha for her enduring friendship – and not to mention the wonderful gift of a book, written in Cypriot dialect, of kalikantzari stories.

Livia Filotico for bringing me into the world of folklore storytelling. Daniel Morden for his myriad tales, wisdom and craftsmanship. All the TellYours gang: you not only helped me hone my skills, but sparked this ongoing exploration of my heritage.

Ian Wong, Laura Sampson, Sam Enthoven, Catt Mott, Dan Coxon: my earliest readers. Your feedback and encouragement was a blessing. Ian, Laura and Sam, let's tell spooky stories again soon.

Laura Shanahan for the expert editing – I owe you so much. The rest of the brilliant Fairlight team, for all their talent, feedback and hard work in shaping this book and getting it into your hands: Louise Boland, Rebecca Blackmore-Dawes, Daniela Ferrante, Sarah Shaw and Lizzie Vascenko. Christina Webb for the copy edits and Gary Jukes for his proofreading. Sam Kalda for his stunning cover illustration and Sara Wood for the slick design.

The many groups dedicated to photos and memories of old Cyprus. You gave me a reason to visit Facebook, and enriched my work.

Friends old and new, booksellers, colleagues, fellow creatives: your support has meant the world. Together, we'll get through this.

Mum, Rosie, Nicky, Chris, Charleston and Kyoto: for your love, security and that sense of home.

Finally, the people who sprinkled my childhood with tales of the kalikantzari. You made the real extraordinary.

Book club and writers' circle notes for the
Fairlight Moderns can be found at
www.fairlightmoderns.com

Share your thoughts about the
book with #AGoodYearNovel